THE HOUSE ON HIGH BRIDGE ROAD

Part Two of The Road From
Here To Where You Stay

THOMAS T. KEMP

authorHOUSE®

AuthorHouse™
1663 Liberty Drive
Bloomington, IN 47403
www.authorhouse.com
Phone: 1 (800) 839-8640

Published by AuthorHouse   02/05/2015

ISBN: 978-1-4969-6919-4 (sc)
ISBN: 978-1-4969-6920-0 (e)

PREFACE

February, 21 1972
Cuyahoga Falls, Ohio

"Thomas, Thomas:
J. Edgar Hoover, Director of the F.B.I. must go."

This note and ten thousand dollars in fifty dollar bills were in an envelope with no post-mark, left in his rural mail-box. Thomas, Thomas had been the code name President Lyndon Baines Johnson had giving to him back in 1962 when he commissioned Thomas to seek out and destroy the killers of John F. Kennedy. Johnson was somehow sure, that Lee Harvey Oswald had not acted alone in the assassination of Kennedy. "Find them Thomas, make them pay an eye of an eye, a tooth for a tooth and death to a murderer." he said.

Richard Nixon was President now and Johnson, in poor health was retired on his ranch in Texas. Thomas was swayed that this note did not come from LBJ, and he knew he may never know who sent it. As he walked to the house on that dark winter evening he knew one thing, someone wanted Hoover dead and it had to be someone who knew his code name. Thomas was introduced to Nixon by Johnson on Nixon's inauguration day in 1969. If you could call it an introduction, Thomas was hurried into the WHITE HOUSE past everyone by Johnson himself; no one questioned the President as he stampeded his will over everyone even glancing at the young Marine and himself.

Thomas had his own reasons why he did not like Hoover. As far back as he could recall he did not trust the Director of the FBI. He had discovered items in the period he sought out the murders of the Kennedy brothers that had left him with the assurance that, the Director knew more than he was ever going the share with the American people. J. Edgar Hoover was in many ways the most feared man in Washington D.C. The chief reason being, he knew so much and had the FBI under complete control. With the FBI as a resource he had the "dirt" on every other position of power. Thomas thought Hoover was more than likely one of the most protected men in Washington. In some ways he was, but normally, he had only one agent assigned to protect him at home. After all, who would try and kill the Director of the FBI

Years before, Thomas was sure that Hoover even knew what Thomas looked like and was doing at the request of President Johnson and that at times he was being watched by Hoover's secret FBI too. For over forty years now Hoover sat at the top of one of the world's greatest organizations for gathering domestic intelligence. Only one President, Harry Truman, spoke out harshly against Hoover. Truman once said, "We want no Gestapo or secret police. The FBI is tending that direction. They are dabbling in sex-life scandals and plain blackmail J. Edgar Hoover would give his right eye to take over, and all congressmen and senators are afraid of him".

Hoover must go! Who would accept the insane task of stopping his career and life?

Thomas thought Hoover was more than likely one of the most protected men in Washington. In some ways he was, but normally he had only one agent assigned to protect him at home. After all who would try and kill the Director of the FBI?

Someone different or new to the neighborhood Hoover lived in would be tagged and noticed right away. Even covering the home Hoover lived in would draw attention to a new arrival driving though at night or during the day. Yet, Thomas's first concerned was the thought of the sniper and his rifle perched in some hide. There waiting to get a glimpse of Hoover walking to his waiting car or coming home at night. The night was always Thomas's friend, he moved well in the mysterious absents of light. Make the killing on the low tide of a spring night, Thomas thought and let it be a moonless night too. As much of nature and its elements had to be with Thomas when death came to call out Hoover.

Present Day:

The phone in my pocket started its riotous chiming and startled me to a consciousness of sorts.

"Hello this is Thomas Kemp."

Come back now, Thomas, I thought. I needed to be in the present. Someone wanted me.

"Thomas, this is Terrace. Tell me, have you started on your new book yet?"

My mind went shifting from the present to what I should be doing for the future. I had agreed to write another book and Terrace was my new driving force in my old nylon sail. She was my editor and maybe my next publisher. She was from the West and I had never seen her, but like the wind I felt her pushing at the mast and helm of my ability.

"Make sure you keep me steeped as you start and remember if there is a time for me to keep you straight it's in the beginning. Now tell me have you started to write today?"

My cherry Grandfather clock struck ten times and her accent did not trail off. Gee what did I get myself into this time? Did I have another book? Yes…but for some reason I was old enough to know this time the story was bigger than the times I have live though…1944 till the present. This book could shake the seats of power on the East Coast. Getting up at 0600 I had already faced the fact my septic tank pump was not working, but I needed daylight to change to a spare. The two horses needed put out to the front pasture and watered. The furnace man called for the new addition project I had started. I needed to start on the book and Mrs. Windy Terrace was blowing in my right ear. I had to smile…yes, I have started the book and that was a reminder of these words I had written to myself some time ago:

"These days I hear the time breathing besides me.

I am standing out of time but the walk of time reminds me of my mortality.

The Sun is approaching the distant cold star Saturn and my breath is freezing when I feel it… time's heartbeat.

Men and women can only come together in peace when there is hope for unity.

Love filling the imperfections and distances of view with deep understanding.

We are not able to recognize the pain of other creatures if we are not one.

She is suffering of separation as much as you are. She lost your words of her soul and gained the daily struggles and realities.

They don't trouble her as much as you do.

There is still a gap in her heart of missing you, hidden in her far forgotten desires.

Is she able to accept the truth and be open to you? I don't know.

There is always a part of cruelty in the mind of lost lovers. Will there ever be peace between them?

Take her by her hand, sometimes, in your dreams. She needs your loving touch.

For a minute in time there was a chance…"

There was a chance my feelings reached someone far beyond my fingertips. My words and thoughts started and tried to touch her soul. What my languor and stillness would never know without speaking. A face of unequaled beauty looked at me in quiet from a sweatshirt and shared some history, at least almost wanting too. Then on Saturday a red moon crossed the early morning sky and, the frost Sun came for a few hours to take hold for another day. When evening came all my fingers were polar, this old heart slowed down. There was nothing else to say. The chance was missed.

Yet I knew there was a way, there was something we had shared. There was a sense of value. You did not realize you were picking up a book to read a story about value did you? Even one's curiosity is of value, but you know that. A plumber adds value to your home with a bathroom renovation. A good cook adds value to your meal. Some of us even know the value of a good story. So, across the nation and parts of the world women and men will pick this book up and I want them to get value. Hours of the kind of entertainment that only a good book brings to you in an airport or while on vacation, maybe curled up by a fireplace. Yes, I have been told I have become a writer, a teller of a good story. Pause for me a minute after reading this! For a minute in time take the chance and let my words touch you. Let me add some value to your life. Did you know one of the frailest flowers, the red Crocus, is ground to a powder and then used in polishing?

Grapes from Chile, cell phones from China and vodka from Russia are everywhere. The world has to change, but do readers of books? Did you ever think about writing a book? Or sat down and tried to organize your thoughts what you wanted to write about? Did you have notes or do an outline? Now-a-days they call it a spreadsheet. Was there something you thought could enthrall your audience that only you could write?

Keep reading! Try this story on! Walk with me along the valley floor next to the Blue Stone River. Let me show you things long forgotten and tell you stories about the men and women who came this way two-hundred years ago. Look! See that stone over there next to the pile of washed gravel and the hillside? A woman like you stooped to fill her deer skin water bag. And, there waiting, in the cleavage of the rocky walls was a man very still and silent. As she bent over to gather the water with her hand, a brook trout swam into her water bag. The silent man almost started to laugh from the stillness of his alcove as he watched her surprise. He maybe would have, if he had not also seen from the corner of his eye the large black bear coming slowly up behind her. She turned and in one movement of the daytime second, both the bear and the man fell together atop that stone, the one over there. Was it in protection she pulled her knife and stabbed at the belly and broke her long blade on the stone top? Both bear and man rolled across the tan deerskin bag and freed the silver brook trout. It swam away free that day."

"Don't stop there...what happened? Come on, tell me?" She spoke out to me."

"A little downstream the river bends, turns from white water to blue. Do not be afraid when I tell you both the fish and the bear won that day. It was long ago, but did I paint the picture for you with my words?"

Thomas T. Kemp

When I was nineteen and wounded the first time I was flown back to the states and rushed into surgery for a number of repairs. About the end of the first week of laying very still, for some reason I was moved into a private room about 2300 hours. The on call duty officer a woman nurse paid me a visit at midnight. She did not speak, but she put her cold hand on my very warm foot. Then slowly as she watches my eyes she moved her hand up my left leg until she reached the other private parts. My response should have been vocal, my body could not move. Slowly she uncovered my body by brushing away the white blanket. Next, she pulled up my hospital dressing gown and by that time I was at attention as a good handsome wounded Marine could be.

Without my permission or words only my cock gave its permission and she went down on me. Night after night it happened and yes I started to get stiff when the door opened. Then early one evening I said something to the male medic. She did not come in that night and I knew it was not her night off. I was so geared to her touch I got hard thinking about her and masturbated at mid-night.

Now, all these years later, with the help of the VA I know why I never trusted women. Why, I had so many affairs and looked for love in the hourglass of sex. I have no idea why you are the way you are, why you want me to write. I have no idea as to why my ex-wife would not let me be who I came to be or why I tried to make a woman happy romantically. All I know is I liked you showing an interest in my writing and me. But I do not think I can be a friend. When I finish the book I will offer it to you first. If you want at that time to peddle the book that is great. If not I understand, I am going to write it my way and I will try to edit the best I can...but you will get what I can do. But, I have only one way to do things and that is who I have become. I am an old man with a story to tell.

CHAPTER ONE

Akron, Ohio July 16 1996

Thomas Camp sits quietly on a bar torn stool at Fred's restaurant, sipping his black coffee and dreading his flight to Paris tomorrow morning. Ever since he was shot out of the sky in a helicopter during the Vietnam War, he has hated to fly. He received a letter a week ago and he promised himself he would go to Paris. The letter was from Jewelko, his Vietnamese lover when he was in the war 30 years ago. There, in Paris, he would meet his twin children, a boy and a girl, that Jewelko just told him about. Jewelko had her reasons for waiting until now to tell him, but he could only speculate as to what they were. She had betrayed him, almost killed him when he was 20, but he forgave her, since it was wartime and war turns people into people they shouldn't be. Back then, he was ordered to kill her for the government, but helped instead, to plot her exile to China and then Paris. He knows now it was the right decision, for if he had killed her, he would have killed the two children she was carrying at the time…if what she says is true and they are his children. He forgave her, but wonders if he can trust her.

Their correspondence over the years has been sporadic. She told Thomas, she had recently lost her long-term male companion and Thomas wonders if she is desperate. She was thirty-three years old in Vietnam when he was 20, so now she is in her sixties. Could she sell her soul now as effortlessly as she sold her body then? She was willing to let him die once, why not again? Perhaps the "children" story was a gambit to gain his trust, nothing more. There are still many wealthy, influential people who if they know what he knows, would want him dead, if for nothing more than revenge.

1

Jewelko herself was not going to meet him in Paris; she said she wanted him to remember her as a poetic lover, not an old woman. She told him her children wanted to meet their biological father. They have seen pictures and heard stories, but want to meet their father face to face. His suffering builds and he searches his pocket for his Tums....

"Hey, Fred! Where's my omelet, I'm dying out here!"

"Do you want it done, Thomas, or do you want it...now?"

Fred Spencer, owner of Fred's restaurant in Akron, Ohio, is no ordinary chef. After attending culinary school in Washington, DC, he cooked at CIA Headquarters in Langley, Virginia. He bought the restaurant when he returned home. The prior owner couldn't wait to sell the old stoves and beat-up rooms of stiff-backed wooden booths and worn-out stools. The 1960's woolen carpet used to be bright red, but now it was muddy dark brown. The wallpaper was from the late 1950's and the pictures dated back to the 40's, which lured the reflective customer-base the restaurant needed to stay above water. To say the place needed updating was kind. Many non-nostalgic patrons spoke of gasoline and a match, but the food was all a man could eat in one sitting and it was good.

Fred's restaurant is proof that good food unifies. The construction workers and city-work crews found Fred's first, then came the college students, businessmen, school teachers, city leaders and the hospital staff from Summit Health Systems. Fred had a junkyard-sized gold mine and he knew it. So did the CIA and FBI, but it wasn't the liver and onions or the Freddie Burger they were trying. Fred's became the gathering place and one of the most unrecognizable sources of information exchange in the city.

Thomas was waiting for his information source to arrive. The phone call he received had been hushed and urgent, but the informant is late and this is adding to his irritation. A young "skinhead" enters the restaurant and all heads turn his way.

Thomas recalls a story he heard about the day Fred's got held up. Fred was standing behind the counter next to the cash register when three high school punks, apparently high on drugs, busted in and began terrorizing the customers. One of the punks in a black ski mask held Fred at gunpoint while he emptied the cash register into a plastic garbage bag. Another punk beat an old woman away from her purse and left her lay unconscious and bleeding on the floor. The third punk, nervous and armed with a shotgun was guarding the door. Fred sensed they were out of control and the situation would turn lethal. He noticed the punk guarding the door could not keep his eyes off of the food, so offered him a donut. At that moment, the plastic garbage bag slipped out of the masked one's hand spilling quarters all over the place; discharging the gun he was holding and shooting down a 1955 fake, stained-glass light which fell on the patrons at table 4. The hungry punk was still nodding "yes" when Fred reached into the donut box, pulled out a 9mm pistol and shot all three of them in less than three seconds. The entire place went from a moment of stilled silence to a clapping roaring auditorium as the echo of the last shot was fired. Then, as if he had done it many times before, Fred blew across the smoking barrel and the place went wild.

In the courtroom months later, 30 different accounts of the story were printed and Fred was found "not guilty" of even manslaughter. After the killings, those who know Fred see strain in his many faces when a stranger comes in, and Thomas sees the strain in his face now.

"Here's your omelet Thomas and not I'm not putting it on your tab, unless you put it in your will that when you die I'll get paid and make sure my lawyer gets a copy!"

Even though Thomas is not a stranger, Fred senses danger when he walks in. Fred is certain he works for "the company" because he is too alert and his senses are always on "stand-by", even while drinking a cup of coffee or chatting about the weather. Fred knows what the death mask looks like and he sees it on the face of Thomas. In fact, Thomas and Fred see death in the face of each other—or perhaps it is strain.

This morning, Thomas, in an effort to calm his nerves, flirts with one of the waitresses. Taking both of her hands into his own, he kisses them saying, "You have the prettiest hands in Akron." She smiles warmly, "So, where are you off too all dressed up--or have you no place to go?"

"I'm going to France tomorrow, want to come along?"

Thomas, knowing how young she is, waits for her cheeks to blush. It appears in an instant along with the disappearance of her smile. "I don't think so Thomas!"

Pulling her hands out of his, she stomps away, almost too good to speak to him the rest of the day. Fred comes over with his "stern face", which is usually reserved for Thomas, "Stop trying to make it with my girls, Thomas."

Fred's wife once told Thomas she is amused when Fred calls the waitresses "his girls". He understands why she doesn't feel threatened. Debbie has been a beauty all her life and knows Fred rarely looks twice at other pretty faces and curves. Thomas and the other men look, until Debbie walks in with their four kids. The waitresses return to the wings and let the real beauty queen take charge of Fred.

"Oh, yea, I see Fred's angels."

Thomas says with a grin then looks up at the only thing new in the place, a color TV tuned to The Headline News from CNN. About that time the old outside steel door with four locks on it opened. A tall thin man came in and walked right over and sat next to Thomas. He was dressed like any other workman, only he was carrying a manila folder, the kind that flapped over and had a small string to hold it closed. He ordered a coffee and before he was finished with it, leaving as fast as he came in, he pulled a dollar bill from his wallet and left it on the counter. Thomas lifted the dollar bill and replaced it with four quarters. He looked at it and noticed the words in red ink, "Flight 800."

In a few minutes he picked up the manila folder and looked over at Fred, who was talking with someone before he left too. Thomas had no way of knowing who would be the drop man, who would bring the information he needed. He did know, the place and time for the drop, and that it would be via a manila folder. He did not expect the code word would be his flight number to Paris.

CHAPTER TWO

New York City July 17, 1996

Stagnation is death! Tonight, the warm water along the East Coast is fairly calm. With each lapping wave, the tide moves a billion mosquitoes, which take off and land in the gentle inlets and pools of stillness. The warmth invites them to come and rest, to be devoured by the hospitable fish. The scorching orange sun has already inched its way toward the nested, cool-green spaces of the western sky; like it is in a hurry to move away from the coastline. To the south, sticking almost out of the sea is the massive towering city of New York. And there, built on domesticated garbage, the debris of millions of people discarded for two hundred years, sprawls John F. Kennedy Airport. Hundreds of thousands of people make their way along the endless ribbons of concrete, to and from the overworked flight center. All day, hundreds of planes take off and land; at least once a week, miraculously so, when the antiquated equipment in the control towers fail the overstressed air-traffic controllers, who every minute cross 600 souls with 600 others.

The anguished voice of the ticket attendant at the red-and-white, TWA concourse, resonates through the overhead speakers: "Ladies and Gentlemen may I have your attention please. It seems that Flight 800 has been over-booked. Anyone volunteering to take the next flight to Paris in the morning will be given one free domestic flight ticket. I am sorry to say if we don't have enough volunteers, I will be forced to use your check-in time as the requirement for boarding passes."

Arlene Stuyvesant, Cable TV's answer to the Animal Kingdom, beautiful, youthful and approaching middle-age, bounds up to the counter with her customary hurried walk. The eyes of a hundred other would-be passengers follow her. Everywhere she goes cameras flash and people stop her for her autograph. She has almost established an empire with stuffed-toy replicas of the animals she has brought from native habitats to the television screen for millions of viewers. Her company is one of the very first to use the growth of personal computers, the magic of interactive CD's and the growing miracle of the Internet to teach children about the animals of the world. She is one of the most recognized women in the world.

"Listen here, I have to be on that plane, I am taping a show in France and there is no way I can be delayed another twenty-four hours." Her reasons are never completely heard, since her voice is muffled amongst the 200 other reasons given. One voice spoke saying, "This isn't fair, and we have been waiting six months for this!" Another voice, perhaps a prophet, said, "Americans are always in such a hurry! God gives everyone twenty-four hours to spend a day. For the starving and oppressed, it is too much, for the rich it is not enough." A stranger taps the man speaking on the shoulder and says, "A rich man is one who learns how to convert excess time into excess self worth."

Arlene learned at a young age how to manage her time and in so doing, increased her self-worth and wealth.

The flight attendant, smiling, plays god over the travelers one more time. "I need two more volunteers to take the morning flight. Arlene Stuyvesant and Thomas Thomas, please pick up your new boarding passes!" Before he could put the microphone down, Arlene, in his face, goes into orbit around him.

"What! I must be on this flight! I have camera crews waiting for me in Paris and it is going to cost me a lot of money for some stupid ticket to Nashville!" Arlene's arms are flying, even though she can't.

"I'm sorry; we based this on your arrival time at the ticket counter." The flight attendant, only a few weeks out of training but an ex-solider from the Gulf War, is more concerned with the next threat he perceives coming

6

from his right. Thomas is leaning on the counter with his hands flat on the plastic counter top. This simple gesture, palms down, is "non-hostile" in body-language-speak and the attendant smiles at him.

"Yes sir, are you Thomas Thomas? TWA will have you on your way first thing in the morning and you can redeem this pass for a round trip ticket anywhere in the continental USA. I am sorry it, was a fair draw."

Arlene stops talking on her cell phone, puts her pocket recorder to her mouth and obtrusively at the attendant says, "I am sending an invoice to the President of TWA and you will reimburse me the cost of this mistake." Expecting a reversal of the decision, she hesitates a moment with the recorder held to her mouth. Thomas reaches over and pulls her hand with the recorder to his lips.

"It's no use lady." Arlene turns to the calm face of Thomas, who holds her hand a little longer. Another camera flash highlights Thomas' four-sided figured jaw and lively blue eyes, as someone takes their picture together. Flustered, she says, "What do you mean?"

A burst of excitement engulfs her when Thomas points her finger to the small print on the ticket.

"On your ticket, there is a disclaimer, nothing you can do." Thomas slides her hand on the counter next to his. Pulling away, she looks at the ticket and throws it at the attendant, "Take this ticket and put it where the sun doesn't shine!"

The attendant quirks, "What about your free domestic ticket?"

"I don't need free--I need to get to Paris. Give it to him; I'll never fly this airline again!"

Thomas, enjoying the flush on Arlene's face replies, "You're giving the ticket to a man who hates to fly. No thanks...Miss?"

"Stuyvesant, Arlene Stuyvesant, but you know who I am."

"No, I'm sorry, but I don't know you."

They start walking away and Thomas denies knowing her again and then a third time. Arlene, her ego thinking this impossible asks, "Don't you watch television Mr. Thomas?"

"No, I'm not much of a TV person. I do like vodka this time of evening, care to join me?"

She thinks she had better not let this opportunity pass, she knows she has seen this hardy man before. After a short walk to the nearest small wayside bar along the concourse heading back to the main part of the airport, Arlene points to a sign directing them toward the VIP lounge. Thomas smiles at her, indicating a "no thanks". A group of twenty or so Sheik Indians is standing half-in and half-out of the six-foot doorway, as if looking for a restroom sign beacon. Thomas doesn't want to go through the crowd blocking their way.

He knew with old senses of manhood that Arlene's eyes were searching his face for the answer to the truth he already knows. They met by chance years before. Thomas, over the chatter of the tour guide herding the Indians away from the lounge, towards the public rest rooms, leads Arlene into the bar. They slide onto the leather seats of the last booth.

The television at the end of the bar is turned up much too loud to talk, so they sit in silence until a suntanned waitress with hair to her waist comes over to take their order. Thomas waits for Arlene, guesses she'll order a gin and tonic.

"Vodka Martini." Arlene says without even looking at the girl. Thomas catches the waitresses' eye and holds it while he orders.

"Vodka and cranberry, crushed please." The girl smiles a little too much for her upcoming tip and goes off to get their drinks. Thomas makes a mental note to ask her to turn down the TV. Arlene looks up from her purse, and gives up trying to organize it.

"So, why did your mother name you Thomas Thomas?"

Thomas studies Arlene's attractive face and looks a little deeper into her warm, yet somehow dangerous, eyes.

"I don't know, I never asked her."

The drinks come and the ice begins to melt. They like each other's company, have nowhere to be, so they order another drink. The waitress starts to bring the drinks to them but suddenly turns white. Her eyes swell up and she drops her tray and money change box. Two soldiers nearly fall over each other trying to help her.

"OH NO!" Her lips form the words silently, until her brain catches up. She screams, hushing the room. All eyes follow hers outside the observation window where fire engines and ambulances race to the smoking fiery debris of the airplane that just took off minutes before.

The Sony TV blares into the silent room, "Our CNN affiliate in New York is telling us there has been unconfirmed reports out of Kennedy Airport and that a Flight 800, TWA 747 bound for Paris France, has disappeared from radar, east of Long Island minutes ago. We are already receiving reports that a plane blew up and has fallen into the Atlantic. Stay with CNN for more about this tragedy, wait, yes, it is confirmed, a TWA 747, Flight 800 has crashed miles out in the Atlantic."

Arlene, shaking, feels Thomas's hand on hers. The rest of her is numb. Millions and millions of thoughts are charging the room, the Airport and the country. Thomas claims two of those thoughts, "I was supposed to be on that plane and it blew up!" and "Terrorism!"

Within moments, every television station in the country was speculating what went wrong and how could this happen. Close to the canyon walls off the Atlantic coastline, Thomas sees the Angel of Death hiding her smiling face in the deep sea.

It appeared as if the airplane had both wings blown off. An eyewitness had seen a fireball falling somewhere off the coast of Long Island. Whatever happened? Both of them sat in shock as they realized both were just spared.

Arlene spoke first, "I remember you now. Death follows you wherever you go. She must love you." Her disposition suddenly changes and the bartender and other patrons glare at her when she yells, "Hey, I was suppose to be on that plane! I deserve a free drink!"

Thomas was studying Arlene's hands, nice and warm. She stunned him with her remark. If cold hands indicate a warm heart, what do warm hands mean? Her cold and cutting demand most likely came from shock; he could not believe she could be that heartless and self-centered. The danger he saw in her eyes earlier overcame the warmth he had imagined. Was he like a mosquito, risking his life for a warm place to land?

Arlene pulls her hands out of his and begins searching and meandering for everything on the tabletop. Her fingernails are plain, nothing fancy or loud. She is five foot seven or eight with short blond hair, touched up some to hide the gray. Her skin's too soft and smooth for a woman her age and her body screams to be touched. Arlene has enough ammunition to lure most men and Thomas senses she uses it.

Later that night, she proved him right. She sent her driver home and they wound up on her attractive couch in the middle of her television show's sound stage office. Although he knew, he asked whom she was to be able to afford her own driver and limo but didn't wait to find out as their bodies linked.

"My god man, don't you know I am Arlene Stuyvesant? I met you at Jackie Kennedy's house years ago; I lived right below her. You were some sort of repairman, but I knew the minute I saw you, you were not a fix-it man, at least not in that sense of the word. God does provide for us does he not, furnishes us with our daily bread and such. Look what He brought me tonight!"

Arlene purred and rubbed her leg up and down his, "You sure know how to fix me, baby."

Thomas, having had enough of her patronizing, was unyielding to her request to spend the night. He got up, dressed, and started to leave. Arlene bounds from the large poster canopy bed as if she is a thirty year old and sets herself firmly in front of the door. Wanting a chance for at an armistice she says, "At least let me call you a cab and have someone take you home. It is dangerous out there this hour of the night for someone Death loves."

"Have someone take me home? My home is in Ohio but I promised I would go to Paris to meet my children and I am going tonight."

Oil and jet fuel will kill almost anything living near the surface of the water. Surprisingly, little was floating towards the beaches, to the warm places mosquitoes come to rest for the night. Close along the shoreline, a small pleasure yacht was motoring south of the city. The Statue of Liberty, lighting the way to freedom for millions of others, watches it pass by. Four men squat on the shoreline, mumbling to each other, scratching through bits of debris deposited there earlier that evening.

CHAPTER THREE

July 18 1996

On the morning news the dialogue was distressing about the plane crash. The NTSB and the FBI were all being called together to investigate the downing and deaths. Thomas was sure that Gretchen Hollowware, an old friend from the FBI who worked now for the State Department for terrorism, would be in the City soon.

This morning the airport seemed more of a mess than the night before. Thomas thought about and then fought back his mind's request to stop and have a couple of vodka and cranberry juices. Just a few feet inside the terminal he recognized the Mayor of New York City giving an interview to the news media, saying something about international terrorism. Well, maybe it was terrorism; then again, maybe that was just one of many possibilities. It might have been the act of a surrogate passenger boarding or an act of a personal survivorship. It may even have been a plot directed at Thomas. It may have been an accident of some sort with the thousand and one systems of the giant plane. He knew one thing for sure. He was going to make his next ticket arrangement with a "new" name, even if still on a TWA flight. He had to get to Paris. The next flight out of Kennedy would not be until later in the evening. Well, he thought, maybe I will have vodka, or two.

At 12:30 PM, he looked over the top of the booth he was sitting in and watched as the limo driver for Arlene Stuyvesant came toward him. The man was in his late sixties or early seventies; he was shorter than Thomas was, he was in better shape, but with thin white flowing hair. Pulling an envelope from his spotless inside coat pocket, he handed it over, by laying it on the table.

"It's from her to you sir." Thomas picked it up and noticed the envelope not sealed and only folded.

The letter read: "Thomas, Nice things about Limos, some have laptops and printers. I decided not to go to Paris but to call and have my boys come home with me. I picked them up on the way over to the airport to find you. They brought me Portuguese bread from the Nantucket bakeshop, flour-dusted and fresh--sorry you missed it...the bread that is. So I'm here now in my office, inhaling the wonderful smell of yeast, feeling good and bad at the same time. Yes, I have two small sons but no spouse, their father lives out on Nantucket Island.

I don't think I will ever recover from the tragedy of the plane crash. I think my X would have liked it if I had been on the plane. I'm grateful to whatever force there may be that I was spared, but I feel guilty I was spared. Why was this privilege extended to me and not to the others?

I remember the "prophet" saying we are all given 24 hours a day to spend, but it is apparent that one day, we will cash in early. I was granted another day and for this day, I feel joy and sadness.

Feeling good and bad is a condition I find myself in often. Perhaps it is a prerequisite for serenity, feeling the dual nature of all human emotion and ultimately becoming comfortable with that duality. I am trying to hear the words behind your words last night; I know they must be there. You told me you did not want to break my heart, well, fear not—you first must find my heart in before you can break it!

I am trying to figure out whether my desire to give myself to you is selfish or unselfish. I lust for your words and hands and the sound of your voice brings a delicious ache to my breasts and belly. Lust is bearable, but longing is difficult. I do not know what I'm longing for. Perhaps you do, perhaps you sense where my heart is hidden.

You said something last night about a Chinese woman loving you without having or seeing you for years, while raising two of your children. Could I do that... Certainly, but what for? I would like to rub your back, not mend your socks. I would like to cook for you, but I hate doing how you Midwesterners say, dishes. So you went out the door and shut it.

"Well don't let the door hit you where the dog bit you." Don't worry; I am not so secure that I will show up on your doorstep someday without being asked. I could never risk that kind of rejection.

I forgive you everything in advance and will not hold you accountable, but please don't forget me.

Miss you already!"

Looking around as if he were being watched, Thomas folds the letter and puts it in his shirt pocket, and then he sees his old friend. The electric doors responded as she went, opening and closing like a vertical eyelid. His eyes cautiously caught a glimpse of her red hair flowing behind her as she moved, then he turned his head away, not sure if he wanted to be seen by her but then he had to look again. He knew she would be ordered to come to the crash scene. Gretchen Hollowware used to work for the FBI but was now working with the United States State Department. He decided not to let himself be seen by her, but sooner or later he most likely would be.

He wasn't planning to see her until around Christmas. Every year, a week before the holidays, she hosted a very large party. The two of them had been friends since high school. Before he could finish his thought, Gretchen was gone. Following her, trying to catch up, was a host of lesser FBI and government men wearing sunglasses.

Thomas headed for the boarding gate for his dreaded flight to Paris. The security was evident today at the airport and it was a good thing he left his twenty-two in Ohio. He never missed carrying a gun until last night when the plane crashed. Automatically, he reached for the steel collateral before realizing he was in one of the world's biggest airports, where only the good guys would be openly armed and only the bad guys would be willing to die to promote havoc.

Boarding the plane was in slow motion. After the plane started to reach for the sky, it was some time before the stewards started down the aisle with the usual fanfare of coffee, juice and drinks. If you took the time to study faces, you could see that no one engaged another's eyes. Fear haunted the open sky as it did thousands of feet below in the deep waters. Just the same, the 747 headed to Paris and Thomas was off to meet his children from another time, a time in his life he would never get over, the war in Vietnam.

Chapter Four

Looking back, he was happy he made the trip to Paris. The excursion was one week old, after the graduation of his son from the Paris College of Fine Arts, when he learned what drew him there. He wanted to see something in the children that would satisfy his curiosity. He wanted to see the small toes of both of these young adults.

"It's not that I don't believe your mother or my own eyes, it's just that I have three children by another woman, you know that, and each one has what I call a, "Camp toe" feature. All Camp little toes roll outward and have hardly any toenail." He didn't have to ask them to show him their toes since both were in the habit of wearing the clothing of Southeast Asia. Their open-toed, rubber tong slippers were the same style whose prints in the mud on a jungle trail sent chills down his back 34 years ago, in South Vietnam.

Thomas recalled instantly, there had been a gunfight and somehow his small squad of men was separated from him. At the time he was sure it was a misunderstanding due to the language barrier but later he realized it had been the simple mistake of going too far before circling back to the spot where the firefight took place.

Right before the attack, Thomas told the six men, "If we meet up with anyone, don't stand and fight, cover fire for one another and withdraw then make a circle and come back here in one hour. Thomas knew as much as the Viet Cong did about setting up ambush points, he also knew that there was not going to be anyone waiting for any length of time in one spot. As the squad of men inched their way forward on the narrow path, the jungle sounds started to die off. The last sound they heard before the guns open fired on them was no sound at all, then the "rat-tat" of the small arms of the enemy and a grenade or two broke the silence.

Just as planned, the others withdrew and Thomas covered for them. He waited, trying to hear cover fire behind him but there was none. He saw a set of black pants and rubber tongs from where he was laying. He fired a little above them and the green plant was not shielding enough to stop his bullet from killing the small man. Then on his left, another flash of black moved in his direction. He fired again and the force of that bullet threw the man back on the ground, revealing the bottoms of his sandals and a logo in English saying, "Goodyear Akron, Ohio.

Thomas turns his thoughts back to Arlene. He phoned her when he returned from Paris because they share another time in his life he would never get over. Getting her voice mail box, he left the following message, I am in New York, would like to see you. I will come by your office at ten PM.

Later at ten, she opened the massive doors to the offices of her cable television empire. He watches her eyelids close tightly as he whispers, "How do I say this any simpler? Do you know a ray of light that is so strong that it could still the illumination coming from your face right now? You are satisfied with my touch—I know that. My voice and words that I'd wrapped up so carefully, seem rusted and yet . . ." His lips stopped moving as the words dried up, their work done.

His sentiments and then his body scooted back. The large, golden earrings she was wearing were dangling on the green-and-cream cradle, in the tub where her head rested. She took off her rabbit fur coat. Her exposed body started to shake, hips moving from side to side as if she were sifting off the flour from some older time of stonehearted love.

By six AM they had travelled to her home, while her driver sped along. By seven both were lodged in her sunken bath. There her head moved like a metronome ticking back and forth as his words; running with the warm water, washed her insides of lust and passion. Thomas, needing a break from the heat in the bathroom, moved towards the door.

Scowling, the little lines above her lips were revealed as she tried to whisper, but immediately became too loud; "Thomas come back here!"

Her time under flowing water was finished, though she promised herself some more later that day. Right now the dry taste of old age and body heat was searching for a cold drink of juice, so she added, more softly, "I need something to drink, please bring some juice back with you."

The water was about to turn cool in the bath. Even an eighty-gallon hot water tank could not serve her tonight. Bracing her thin tan beautiful legs against the wall, her back rested against the warmth and pressed toward the tub. Splashing a little, the water gathered at her shoulders and gently tried to lift her small breasts. Flattening her feet to point to the ceiling and imprinting the steamy shower wall, she wondered, how much more could I take? How much more do I need tonight? How much more do I want? Without responding to her questions, her feet slid down the rose tile wall and sunk below the shallow water.

Thomas, a soft snowy white towel around his waist, felt his bare feet drying, until, in the kitchen, no trace of his movements marked the maple hardwood floors. Pulling both doors of the two oak-covered Sub Zero refrigerators sitting next to each other, he laughingly sang the refrain, "Old mother highborn went to the keyboard, but there is no juice in sight." She could not hear his tune. There was plenty of ice, plenty in the freezer section—that was about all there was! So, picking what looked to be an old blue glass jelly jar, he filled it with ice and water from the stainless spigot and carefully wiped the excess water that spilled over the lip.

Walking back through the house to the airy open bedroom, he found her naked, drying her short blond hair with a smaller match to the white towel he wore. As he handed the jar of ice water to her, she looked inside disgustedly.

"No, juice?"

"None to be found."

"That damn woman, I've told her a hundred times to keep juice in the refrigerator for me!" She drank down two, maybe three large gulps, before placing the jar on the nightstand and putting her hand out to him. When he was close enough to the monarch-size bed for her to reach the end of the towel, she pulled hard and it fell away. Smiling at her silliness, she readjusted herself on the bed and lay back with her dripping hair using the green and white sheets for a new towel. His retaliation was to pick her feet up and swing her body around to face the headboard. But then he gently took her face, as if made of fine china, and sat smoothing her hair back, continuing his words from the tub; "Your body is so firm, the stern side like soft skin pulled tight over a rocker." He moved even closer, dropping his voice, "I am the man who knows your secret strength. I know how much you always wanted to be . . ."

Quickly putting her hand behind his head, she pulled him to her wet lips. They were almost stoic kisses at first and then she thought about what he had said and she began to trust he did know her secret. Her face gently roamed across his and back again a hundred times before she pulled away. Without missing a breath, he was back at her ear, "I know--it's okay, I understand. I even like the feel of it on my mouth."

"How do you know so much about me so fast?"

Chuckling, he answered, "I watch your show now and you telegraph everything."

"I don't tell of my sexual needs on television--WHICH I don't do!"

"Then stop sometime and watch to see the real beauty of what you say and do out there. You're one of the sexiest women I have ever seen."

"No, I am sorry, I stand up and walk to my mark, I look at the cue card and I say, for the most part, what's printed there. You may be reading a little too much into my performance." With a small smile, though, she closed her eyes while she added, "I do think it's important to tell you this--you make me feel young and sexy." Responding to a long and deep kiss and her words, Thomas quickly moved to rejoin her, only to again go where she was most strapping to talk in slow strategic verses,

"Do you know how much I want to serve your desires tonight? Because of you and your prearranged bath, this room already smells of glory; and my appetite for you is growing. Even the static between us is a pulling at my heart; the touch of your body next to mine stretches me and pushes my wish for all of you. The narrow between your lips, where I want to place my tongue to feel your teeth open up for me, beckons. To know you are responding to my every move, it makes me go slowly, savoring each touch . . . these special private part of yours, I can taste it already melting in my mouth, it has anesthetized me. Let me..." He didn't finish, for she rolled over on top of him.

It was close to five-thirty Sunday morning; close to the time the neighborhood red rooster would make the first sleepy call to the Connecticut village. Outside and down the road, a couple of different dogs barked their hello to each other. A chill went though him as he stopped to listen and look across the lawn. Far to the east, the sun was inching its way across the open Atlantic Ocean. This was much the same way he remembered it had skirted crossing the South China Sea years ago. Hundreds of miles to the northeast, some of the first cracks in the short days of winter were beginning to warm the ice pack of Greenland. Any day now, the icebergs would fall off the ice shelf, begin to sail south, only to get caught in the Gulf current, and then be carried off to England and beyond.

Only here, today, the land lay frozen in the unfeeling hands of winter. Outside, the dock posts and rocks were the only sign that spring was a month away. What heat the day generated. It worked its way down from the top of the post into the rocks to keep the water from freezing solid, it sat next to the lake's edge. Here inside, however, she was very warm and had kicked off the sheets that only minutes ago had covered them. Unconsciously Thomas rubbed his fingers across his forehead. The tiny image in the distant mirror as he got out of bed, reflected some sort of mark there.

Arlene had a nice house; her home, built of wood and stone, sat on a small hill away from town. The stones were as old as the earth and the wood had to be over two hundred years old. It was big and beautiful, painted white with a red roof and blue trim. Each of the eleven rooms had a fireplace. They stood masterfully made up as if to highlight the contact the house had with the earth it sat on. Even the grand front porch, with its two massive rock columns, made a dramatic pronounced nostalgic demand, "Look at us." The gardens of spring, summer and early fall were now private and prismatic. Everywhere, he could see the process of professional gardens that were so unlike his garden back in Ohio. From the bedroom window and the small deck off the bedroom he could see east to the ocean and the endless white cap waves.

Both of them, her first, and then he, surfaced from the origin of life's onward movement, back to the morning and the coming day. There was an undercurrent of orderliness in the home, but in her he felt restlessness and panic as she stood and moved away from the bedroom. In a matter of minutes she came back, wearing a royal blue cotton bathrobe, unbuttoned to reveal her silk underwear that was pulled much too high on her rounded hips. She didn't say a word; just stood there holding two cups of steamy hot coffee in heavy earthen stoneware mugs. Balancing on her left foot, she lifted her right and ran the tips of her toes down the backside of his dark calf muscle. Feeling her mood, he asked, "Are you okay?"

Her lips closed tightly and with a small smile, she responded, "I know a lot of people who think I am inflexible. Many people thought I was going through the change of life years ago."

She changed the look on her face to a dutiful expression until he very gently reached up. Rubbing dry saliva from the corner of her mouth with one finger, he also took a mug of coffee. Then, embarrassed, she also rubbed at the drool, but also searched his eyes, wondering what he had been thinking. Puddles of candle wax had become solid again, but it now lay in many melted shapes of the early morning's ruptured desires.

Starting to dress, he asked, "Oh, why is that?"

She let it go, so he did not press for the answer.

"Will you come back; will I ever see you again? I never know, at first I didn't want to let it make me wonder, but . . ." She cocked her head to the side and moved her eyes blankly to his belt. "I like a man who puts his socks on last and takes them off first." This time she tried to be superficial with her words.

"Arlene, before that night, did you care if you ever saw me again? No, you did not, what is so different now?" He stood holding both of his socks in one hand and his shoes in the other.

"We're different people now because of it, and I didn't know it was this--you--I was looking for. You make me laugh and I respect you. Yet, you seem a child-like male god who understands my reasons for sex and loves me for it...you are mentally strong yet know the meaning of tears." She backed away from his side and both of them looked into the large gold-framed mirror.

"Tears relieve, the perfect stress buster."

"Do you realize how lucky we are? You're right again, but I haven't cried in front of a man since my dad busted my butt as a teenager. Thomas, I want you to come and tape a commercial with me. Oh god, I have a better idea, let's do a show from your house on the mound." Her foot was moving up and down on the inside of his slacks, as she buttoned up his top two buttons.

Thomas focused on the red "X" that he could now see clearly reflected, as he absently, responded, "My house is not on the mound, it's behind it." Where . . . the Angel . . .

This was the second time since the night of the crash of TWA flight 800 that she had mentioned coming to Ohio to visit. Last July as they stood in the VIP lounge watching the CNN report of the crash, they were drawn together by both missing the departure of the plane bound for Paris.

Thomas knew relatively a lot about Arlene and her background; he knew she was Arlene Stuyvesant, the animal world's answer to everything. The perfect woman, she was the number one draw on her own national cable television show about animals. He knew that in television circles she couldn't say she was sorry, never did anymore, and freely admitted she was way too headstrong. The first night they met he knew something was happening when she said, "Ohio, my god, Ohio, that's close to Indiana, I knew you were a Midwestern man."

"Yes, just a normal man."

"If you leave you are not like the normal man I have known. Go on I dare you, go on and leave . . . I'll come to visit with you in Ohio some day or you'll be back here."

He smiled to let her know she was okay before he said, "You're cute but I'm not gratuitous or that easy."

"For god's sake don't call me cute, I am almost fifty! Look Thomas, whatever your last name is, it's not easy for me to talk without a script and about things like animal relationships . . . Oh, forget it." She was getting irate with herself.

"I really understand women like you, honest." He shook his head a couple of times and went out the door, saying "good night" as he closed it in her face.

The second thing that struck him that night was the stale air of New York City. Even at this light hour of the morning, it was easy to find a taxi to take him back to Kennedy Airport. Looking out over the streets, he remembered the last time he had come down this far into Manhattan and to Central Park. It was back in the '70's and he had gone to see Jackie Kennedy after she sent for him. That time he had driven himself. He was crazy enough back then to drive into New York.

CHAPTER FIVE

September, 1946

Arlene Anne Stuyvesant was a many-time-removed grandchild and heir to Petrus Stuyvesant. Her great-grandfather was the first Dutch administrator of colonial America in New York. At that time the Dutch Queen told Petrus, "Either take the job or go to debtor prison." Arlene's family was soon "new world" wealth and became a backer to the "Articles of Confederation." Her family was East-coast aristocracy. Her dad became chairman of the board of directors for one of the largest realty companies in the country, which had been founded by his father.

Arlene was the only child of David and Rebecca Stuyvesant. She was born aboard the British luxury liner Queen Mary, halfway between Gibraltar and New York City. Three days out, early the morning of Labor Day, 1946, her mother awoke her father with the news. The entire trip had been this way. One thing after another had held them up from returning home when they were expected. Her father had to chuckle at first, this millionaire Realtor, thinking his daughter was born on "Labor Day."

Being somewhat of a super-spiritualist she, Arlene's mother thought it was a bad omen when her husband suggested the trip. David wanted to go to Europe and gloat over the condition of the Dutch and German people. As the spirited wind moved across the sea's surface and became more tossed and vengeful, the ship's doctor struggled with Rebecca and her stubborn child. Arlene had entered the birth canal bottom first.

The one and only thing that David recalled years later was how bright and warm it was inside the operating room. Finally with a small straight knife in hand, the doctor cut down through the young wife's belly, as the cold waves slapped against the lower deck portholes. Then placing his white-gloved hands into the young woman's uterus, the doctor pulled Arlene from the innermost depth of Rebecca. Still connected to her mother, he lifted the baby girl up with only one hand in final celebration and placed the child into a waiting cotton blanket held by one of the ship's male nurses. Wrapping the child up, the nurse gave her back to the doctor who then laid her into the arms of the mother. However, the new life could not calm the fear Rebecca felt. For outside the steel bulkheads of the ship, the winds drove the storm harder and moved it up to what sailors call a "gale wind."

The doctor thought for a minute during the caesarian-section operation that he might have accidentally cut Rebecca's bladder. This was a short-lived fear as this was the first operation he had ever performed. When Rebecca's water broke and the three small bleeders were unchecked, he had more to do than he remembered. What really happened went unnoticed during the operation as the doctor started to cut down through the seven different layers of tissue. When he was about to open the womb, his knife slipped enough from his blood-soaked hand to puncture a "pin hole" into the bladder wall. At the time, the bladder was empty. As the seas grew up and the storm raged white then dark, a small amount of urine was seeping into the body's cavity next to the surgical incision. The infection was almost unstoppable in the mother by the time Arlene was one day old.

Ship's Captain Andrew Miller of the Queen Mary did not have to go to the private luxuriant staterooms of David Stuyvesant to find him. David was holding "court" in the main lounge for anyone who acted as if they wanted to celebrate with him. While he still drank and commemorated the birth of his first child, his first spouse laid filling with a swelling death.

David never recovered from the death of his wife. It was a hard blow to everyone in the family. The service was held in the foyer of the main house where he wanted her to spend her last days above the earth so hundreds of grieving people paraded in and though the house. Even the matron of honor of his recent marriage offered herself to him to ease his pain. He took her into his sister's old bedroom and would not open the door for twenty hours. As the fire department moved to break down the massive door, he opened the bolt and once she stepped out, her husband punched him back into the room--all the way to the rumpled bed.

Arlene's life as a young child was not easy. She tried to learn the ways of one female nanny after another, until she was ten. It was a surprise to her father when she announced to him at Thanksgiving that year that she intended to marry the thirty-one-year-old gardener named Jesse Philip. The very same evening while the gardener said grace over his family's meal his phone started to ring.

"Yes, this is Jesse Philip, can I help you."

Jesse Philip was a small man for the most part. He was five-eight and weighed around one hundred and forty pounds. He had brown eyes and a weathered rugged face. David Stuyvesant thought that Jesse Philip looked like a young Spencer Tracy. Sitting back in his red leather chair, his face was flush with anger. Glaring at the mouthpiece of the phone as if Jesse could see him, he said, "Come to the house! Come right now Philip!"

The butler, John Reeves, was in charge and responsible for the work of the household staff. As in most homes of the wealthy, he did the hiring and the discharging of employees. Reeves had liked Jesse Philip and the work he saw the young man do. He knew Arlene liked Mr. Philip, but, then again, everyone seemed to like him. An added plus he brought to the position, the butler told Mr. Stuyvesant, was that he was married and could live in the gatehouse with his wife and keep an eye on who came and went.

Philip's wife saw the look on her husband's face as he put the phone on its cradle. If something terrible had happened, she wanted to know and spare the blunt remarks her husband might make in front of their children. "What is it?"

"He wants me at the house right now."

"My god, Jesse, what's happened?"

Nervous and with a cold sweat racking his body Jesse said to the servant who opened the door, "I am to see Mr. Stuyvesant. He called and said to come now. Do you know what's wrong?" The old man had no idea what to answer, but scurried off to inform Mr. Stuyvesant that the gardener was there.

Arlene was hiding behind a large red Persian curtain that draped and framed the doorway to the servants' dining- room. When the gardener came to the door and rang the side bell to the kitchen, she was as alarmed as one of the kitchen workers. Arlene ran up the steps to her father's study, trying to find out why her favorite male friend had come on Thanksgiving Day. She was at the side of her father's large cherry desk and started to pick up her mother's gold-framed picture when her father said grimly, "Put that picture down of her and leave! Go to your room and leave me alone!"

How could he know the facts of a little girl's life? He was still sure it was his insistence that his wife have a baby boy that caused her death. What private school or teacher would ever prepare him for the fate he felt he created? It was more than just the dying Rebecca and the wounding of his spirit. Ever time he looked at Arlene, his mind yelled at him to give up and die too.

Jesse Philip had a dozen jobs while he worked his way through the University of New Hampshire at Merrimack Valley. He did everything a young person could do to work and put himself into a position of trust with his employer. After graduating with a degree in horticulture and while he was waiting for acceptance into the master's program, he went looking for a position.

Jesse interviewed at "Steed Farm," the home of David Stuyvesant. He surprised Mr. Reeves with the many letters of patronage he had gathered over the four years of college. There was a letter from the University President and even one from a Jewish pawnbroker in Hartford. The president said his college-furnished home was a masterpiece of gardening and the pawnbroker said, "This boy will surely pay back his debts."

Jesse's father was an ordained minister and the headmaster of a private Christian day school in Hartford and well respected. The butler knew of the school's high standards. His younger sister also taught school there. The last question asked Jesse Philip, "What are your far-off goals?"

He answered, "I want my Ph.D. in horticulture and chemistry and I want to marry my girlfriend, Nancy." That had been five years ago last summer.

The first time Jesse Philip met Arlene, she was five years old and he was twenty-six. It was a warm spring day in April. He had been pruning back a row of blue spruce north of the main house where the sunlight was only directly overhead on them at noon. The rest of the time, the young trees sat in the shade of the house or under the pattern of stately elms. He knew the following winter he would move the trees, transplanting them in a broken, more natural row to the southeast. This was not the time of year to move coniferous trees. He would wait till November, Thanksgiving week.

Young Arlene watched every move he made. As he weeded around the trees, every now and then he would catch sight of her from behind the pilings. The pilings would one day support very large stone granite and wooden walkway deck, for Mrs. Stuyvesant's had planned it years before. The walk was to be sort off a pilgrimage from the main house, and would eventually lead all the way to the beachfront cliffs. A yellow-breasted pine warbler sprang and flew from one of the trees as Arlene came up behind Jesse and pulled at his right shirtsleeve. The bird's flight at first frightened them. Then turning to one another both of them started to laugh. Jesse spoke first. "I know who you are, but the bird scared me."

Laughing out loud Arlene said, "And I know who you are."

"Oh, who am I?" He crossed his arms across his chest holding the pruning shears.

"You're the man who makes things pretty!" Her little voice was clear and her words did not match her size.

"You are very smart for such a small little woman."

"Yes I am, and someday I'll be your helper. Why do you have to cut so much from the trees?"

"Well, I will tell you, if you tell me something first."

"What?"

"Why do you still carry your pillow around with you?" Around the estate it was a topic of discussion and custom to see Arlene with her pillow. Two or three times a day, one of the housekeepers would find and exchange pillow cases. Mr. Reeves had suggested this after someone had tried to cover the pillow with a plastic cover. It was an honest effort to protect the pillow and the child from contact with germs, but the plastic case was soon unzipped and discarded.

"It makes me think of my daddy, soft and warm. Now, your turn, why do you cut the trees?"

He would have thought it was to remind her of her mother, not her father. Jesse Philip had always heard how hard Mr. Stuyvesant was. Every time he had ever seen the man, he always tipped his hat to him; and, for the most part, Mr. Stuyvesant always offered a small little wave back. Mr. Reeves had told him after a staff meeting one day that Mr. Stuyvesant had acknowledged the fine work he was doing and that one wave a day was plenty. He had to think about that for a minute, and then realized he waved every time he saw Mr. Stuyvesant, so he had promptly begun to wave only the first time they met each day.

"In order for a tree to grow straight and for it to look like you want it to, a gardener prunes away parts," Jesse said with a smile. "It is almost lunch time, do you want my piece of apple pie? The apples came from your orchard."

"Yes."

The two of them started walking over to the small open garden house Rebecca had built before the ill-fated trip to Europe. He sat down and helped her up on the white wooden swing. Jesse opened the pail and handed the pie to her and poured her a little tea--not too much, he wanted it to cool quickly and be ready to wash down the pie.

After Jesse married, he and his spouse did move into the gatehouse at the end of the serpentine, granite-chipped driveway. He started to make a routine of packing his lunch and a thermos of sweet hot tea early in the morning. The small barn that housed the garden tools sat at the other end of the estate from the gatehouse. The walk was only about ten minutes, but unlike the other staff, which worked in the house, Jesse felt his lunch was just thirty minutes long. So, he would carry his lunch bucket with him if he were not going to make the trip back.

"I bet my father would like to prune me!" she said, matter-of-factly. He looked over at her but offered no counsel or smile. He waited and watched for her to lick her fingers, then gave her the napkin from the lunch bucket and the thermos cap of tea.

When Jesse walked into the den that Thanksgiving Day, he was sure it was for something of appreciation from Mr. Stuyvesant--maybe the way the gardens had looked this summer and autumn had really impressed him. Of course, he knew he had nothing to do with the brilliant colors. Mr. Stuyvesant was sitting, slumped behind the massive cherry desk. David Stuyvesant turned around after Jesse said, "Yes sir there was something you wanted to see me about?"

His employer never looked up from the papers in front of him while he wrote out a check and handed it up. He offered no reason for the discharge. He said he did not want to wait till Mr. Reeves returned on Monday. He said, "I want you and your kind out of the gatehouse and off the grounds by the following Monday. You will be separated with one month's pay and what every time you have coming for vacation. You will be paid for the Christmas and New Year's holidays. There will be no referral from this house for you, so do not ask at a later date."

Jesse stood there, not sure of what he had just heard.

"That is all, Mr. Philip, please leave now."

Arlene, hiding, rather than going to her room as told, knew that at this very minute she had an aversion for her father in her stomach. The strong associations she felt for both men pulled at her breath and she could not contain herself. She loved her father and knew the warmed touch of his sorrowful nature. She also knew she must openly tell him how much she felt for Mr. Philip, confess the truth to her daddy. In her heart she started to cry silently. "No daddy, don't send him away, he is almost like you, daddy, please no." But she stayed silent, too afraid to let her father see how much she cared for this man who made things pretty.

Jesse Philip stood for a few seconds looking at the pines he had moved four years ago. He would have never seen them from this location had he not been here. Each one of the trees had grown two feet or more in the new space. Tears formed in his eyes as he turned and saw Arlene's feet sticking out from behind the over-stuffed red leather couch. He lowered his head for some reason, like a person who had done something wrong, and walked out of the house.

Nancy Philip could not believe her ears, would not for a minute let him talk about his disappointment. She was too concerned with what the staff would think, after he told her they must move. He didn't know the reason for his discharge, so when she pressured him for an answer he had none. Doubt and mistrust are a malignancy in a marriage; love was no longer manageable. The affinity between one another was torn into patchwork and the marriage soon ended.

When Arlene was elected to it, she sat on the board of directors for the "American Funds for the Arts and Sciences." She was also President of "Petrus Stuyvesant and the Animal Archives of America." All of her life she was a great horse trainer and rode for the United States Equestrienne Olympic Team in Mexico City.

It was during the kind years of her life when she went from one spouse, looking to the next. Then the ambivalent years followed, perhaps created through the sudden firing of the man for whom she had felt her first girlish love. The last spouse, who had a chance, came from an accidental meeting too. At a retreat in the northwestern woods of Washington, she met James Lewis. "Let's Save the Spotted Owl National Club" was meeting there.

James Lewis had just lost his teaching position at the College of William and Mary. He said it concerned his unfair dealing with a female student, not sharing the "small" rumor that he had not held to the policy of not fraternizing with students. Instead, he told Arlene there was no time for a hurried wedding or even an announcement to the families. The two of them were off to the Arctic Circle to check the effects of the permafrost, and to try and discover what an early thaw would do to the sleeping conditions of bear cubs.

By mid January James Lewis knew who he had married--the worlds' animals. To them, she was benevolent. When it came to people, she was nasty. When it came to him, she turned cold! When she walked out of divorce court six months later, she told "People Weekly" the magazine, "For a teacher, the man can't put more than six words together. Do you want to get up? Can you find my shirt? Do you want to sleep? Would you start my car? I'm hungry, are you?" My god, she said, "Men--who needs them?"

In fact, she was fond of closing her television show with this phrase. "Animals are not like mankind; whereas men are all alike, animals are not, animals are ambitious, and eat to live, where men live to eat. Men are, she said, uninspiring beside a male tiger."

She was right for the most part. Men had gone from the wet sandy beaches of France and Italy to the mountains and across the rivers of Europe. In her lifetime, men had laid their hearts next to each other in the frozen hills of Korea, from the wet jungle and water-covered rice patties of Vietnam, to the sand-swept desert of Kuwait. She did not realize that these places had held her captive, as had been the men who walked there. These far-off lands with funny looking animals had held her in place so many times during the course of time.

It seemed as if most men had forgotten about trusting and fairness. Thomas was lucky and knew this was one of the reasons so many men had fallen into the human pit of divorce, for sex had become almost a social frenzy to many men.

A man could be led from the customary protective nature men felt for his loved ones and mate, to dishonor. Guarded compassion now took the place of tender love in the hearts of too many men. Tenderness lay in ruins or in the many places forgotten or never discovered. Most men only thought they knew what a woman needed; it was something they thought that was automatic like the beam from a remote control. Love's warranty, too many men, became snappish and seemed worn, reminding them of the television show where dad always knew best and each man in his heart knew better.

Rather than studying the walk of a woman as she came into the room, rather than trying to understand the looks a woman offered over her glass of milk, at the breakfast table. Men acquired the knowledge of the infinite ways the forward pass flew into the night air, watching Monday night football. Instead of walking with a woman along some shallow riverbed on a spring Sunday morning, men played at manly things. For a man could find very little to fashion himself after, once his own father died. Thomas knew Arlene responded to him for two reasons. He was capable of understanding the melting spring snow off the hillsides and he had himself known a woman's love.

CHAPTER SIX

March, 1967

The cold dead-finger days of winter were passing up the shoreline to the north. The embers in the grand old fireplace were cool, and turned over. There was nothing left to burn or to fire any warmth from the huge hearth. It was time for Thomas to go home and retrace the footprints left in the wet snow. How many were the mile markers he had passed? Airports and seaports of call had dotted his memory with all sorts of logos. Even up to this day, all of them made a difference. How many trips, had he made into the clenched hands of the world?

Now he just wanted to go home; wanted to stand in his own space, sleep in his own bed—there where he habitually ran fingers across the splintered hole in the headboard. It had been three years from the day his old live-in girlfriend accidentally shot at him. Now he wanted to go home to find the next morning and see face to face the beckoning of light as he stood in his own winter garden of stones. Home was where he had learned to speak with the past. It was where he discovered the deep stretching personal mind of the poet.

Words were as important to him as was a woman's hand. The softness and the slowing touch of a word became as much a promise to his mind, as did the brush of some pretty lady's hair to his senses.

It was also at home in the garden, where he grew older and noticed the very tall ladder of evil reaching upward into the top circles of society. What once had been so unheard of in our big corporation was now as common as the mugger in the street was. Only now the hype spooned to the public is, "well everyone is doing it." The thief named decay was holding the country hostage, and our disintegrated people's honor, was not even a concern of this new society.

The masters of the country were changing names. Selfishness and greed propped up most of them. Much of the new wealth was a result of the surge in the stock markets of not only ours, but of five or six countries. The older powers were weakening from fat and age. The results were too hard to imagine, unless you had seen it happen before in history. The poet in his mind would go to those words he has seen written years ago.

"Love will always stretch for its own sake, and mud will always be mud. So, which one fills your life?" This was not the love of empire building or of winning of the West. It was not the quest for the Holy Grail. It was man's desire for power; and history's lesson had taught Thomas, all power is temporary. If all power is temporary, then all real love is permanent.

Arlene's father had been one of these temporary men. His passion for power had started when, as a young man, he witnessed his father's seduction of a young maid in the basement of the mansion house. The as years passed he too, had been drawn into the torrid halls of sexual hell.

Thomas's mind wandered back to the last scene with Arlene. She had opened the heavy wooden door immediately. Her body, wrapped in a white bath towel, and stood against it in silhouette. It was obvious she was not worried anyone would see her, the queen of cable animal TV. Then she took a step or two across the snowy porch and called out, "Call me when you're safe at home?" It was more of a question than a statement. Still, Thomas nodded his head, as he quickly started the car.

After the death of John and Bobby Kennedy as he had been commissioned to do, he sought and killed their killers. There were a few years where he had a wonderful feeling in his heart with poetry. Somehow the scars and bindings of his past wounds healed with each poem he wrote. On the drive back home he relived many of the missions on which he had been sent. Also, there were the ones he undertook for friends and himself. Thomas's thoughts led him to wonder about the accidental crash of Flight 800 back in July. Even after many months, the NATB and FBI still had no way of knowing for sure what had happened. Every piece of salvageable wreckage had been pulled up from the waters off Long Island. Every person who had any interest in the passengers and flight was contacted and interviewed. The mystery remained. "What happened?" Yet, no one ever called him since he was using a phony passport and, oddly enough, no one had called Arlene.

Few people know the rules that govern air flights in this country. One little-known fact is that the government has the right to step in and seize control of every airplane. This type of power is understandable; it serves the idea of the common good, for the security of the nation's airspace and the carrying of air materials must be guarded to protect the interest of U.S. civilians. For a government to take the wealth of its people and, in turn shield them from harm with it had its originality as far back as four thousand years ago in places like China and Egypt. For the most part, back then there was a control for everything--slaves, farming, and commerce. The idea of empire building was old; there was nothing new under the sun.

The daylight sky surrendered to the evening hours. Clouds that looked like the floating flowers of a wedding march vanished. It was dark, not even moonlight. Two hundred and fifty miles, still to go. Thomas's visits with Arlene were becoming too cumbersome, he thought, with my having to drive to her home, every fourth Friday. Right after their third time alone, she gave him a key to a small white cottage. This was but one of the five homes that still made up the estate of her father and his father before him. The cottage sat between her beautiful home and the great house. Arlene's threat to come to Ohio never occurred. She was far too busy. Already her television show had taken her around the world twice. Unlike Thomas, she was never slow to board a plane heading for anywhere. Once during a phone conversation, she told him she was like her father in that way, for traveling was an adventure for her.

After she would come home to America, Thomas loved making love to her, yet the guilt of it never left him. Guilty, for he had lied to her the day they first met, when he told her, he didn't know who she was and had smiled doing it. Now for six months, he felt the line being pulled in and the lie, starting to grow bigger, coming to the surface. Yet, he loved to find himself in her spaces. The only thing he could do was wait...wait while he traveled back and forth to love her body so freely. Then in the shadows of the winter's ember glow, he heard himself once more glibly lie.

CHAPTER SEVEN

Spring, 1997

Thomas was one year old when World War II was over in August of 1945. The large luxury ships, which had been pressed into service carrying troops to Europe, were converted back to ships of beauty for the wealthy. Shortly before the Queen Mary set sail for England with paying passengers, including the wedded Stuyvesant, David had gone down to the city of New York to talk with nine businessmen from around the country. During an early visit to a private men's club off Fifth Avenue, one of his closest friends, Robert Barbet, had bought him a drink and kidded him about his upcoming wedding night. "She will be the last virgin you'll ever have. Do you think it's worth the cost? Just think of those young laps you'll never see up close again. As for me, I am staying single. It was plain to see why; Robert Barbet was close to three hundred pounds and only five foot six inches tall. His face was still young looking, but his hands looked like blown up rubber gloves. What woman would want him to fondle her?

"Ah, think what you like my friend, when the war is over in Europe there will be all kinds of young things to work over. Thousands of girls will do anything to come to America. What do you want, girls from Norway, France, Germany, Poland, what? You see my friend, some of us are looking into bringing many of the younger ones here."

A smile immediately covered his face as his eyes narrowed. Robert's interest was sharpened. From sitting back in his red leather overstuffed chair, he inched his heavy weight forward and snuffed out the tobacco in his pipe with a blunt silver ramrod. "Go on; tell me . . . what is this all about? What are you up to?"

Trains had made Robert's family wealthy. His grandfather was not into the big railroads that ran across the country. No, he was a toy maker, and his trains ran around the bases of Christmas trees for about one week a year. The two boys first met in private boys' school in eastern Pennsylvania. They were not close friends at the time David was buying the services of a fifteen-year-old girl from the local town.

Robert came back to school six hours early on a Sunday morning and discovered David and the girl named Maple in his single bed. Also there in his bed he saw the blood; the fifteen-year-old had given birth. David and the girl both were holding a pillow over the small cries of the baby. Turning around and discovering Robert, David pushed him to the floor and jumped him.

"You say one thing about this and you're a dead kid, understand?"

Robert was as excited as David had been. He felt the small hard-on in his boxer shorts growing. He whispered to David, "It's okay, it's okay, and just let me have her next."

Only an hour or so after giving birth, the baby was dead and the new friends were further tearing the girl. After both of them fell exhausted from the bloody lap of the girl, Maple looked at the dead child; "It was a boy. I'm glad it's dead, I sure wouldn't want it to grow up to be like you two."

In fear she fought back her tears of loneliness, and asked, "What are you going to do with it?"

David looked over to his new fat friend, and smacked Robert on the stomach with his open hand. "Don't you worry about it, no one will ever tell? Have you ever seen what a dead animal on the Parkway looks like after a couple of hundred cars run over it?"

He rolled over, pushed himself up, went over to the small sink, and splashed water over his groin and dried himself. He turned like the animals he loved and met her eyes looking at him.

"I better not get the drip this time either." Maple looked at him with hate.

"You won't!" She said, backing away from his stare.

Early the next hollow sunup, the air was strange and not a leaf shuddered in the trees. A cab pulled up to the outside gate of "Bogart Martin School for Boys" and the two young men, clothed in their school uniforms, got in. David told the cab driver, "Down the Parkway to the city."

Close to town, at fifty miles per hour, David rolled the window down, saying, "Hope you don't mind my rolling the window down, the smoke is going straight into my eyes."

With a sneer for the young "preppies," the driver was looking back through the mirror when the dead baby's body, wrapped in three pillowcases, hit the pavement from the other window. Within an hour, over ten thousand cars and trucks, the first ones trying not to hit the "thing" in their lane, would be rolling their way into the city of New York.

Robert sat back and tried to cross his legs. From the time he had been sucked into getting rid of the baby twenty years ago, he had both feared David and wanted to be around him to prove his own dauntless manhood to himself.

"So David, who all do we know who wants to have their own stable of young European girls, why just girls? I know a few who, in some ways, prefer the company of a young man."

"Well not me, you know me better than that!"

"What difference does it make girls or boys, the same thing would work, if we found them young enough, hell, there is a whole wide country out that window." He pointed with a motion of his hand toward the window and the streets, thirty floors below them. He knew many men around the world who would pay highly to have their own "child bride."

"The difference is it has to be a better kept secret than the 'A-bomb.'"

"Then you need someone like J. Edgar."

"That's not funny." David stopped smiling and quickly got up from his stuffed chair with such force that the chair fell over into a coffee table behind it, spilling his drink everywhere. From the next room an older man appeared with two white towels to blot up the stains on the woolen carpet. David was always making a mess for someone to clean up, Robert thought to himself.

"I'm not trying to be funny. Hell, man, the guys a flamer."

"Yea, who told you that bull? And even if he is, he's also the Director of the FBI! Let him keep catching commies."

"There is a flamer close to Hoover, his name is Warren and he is the Assistant Director, he likes young pretty boys with darker skin."

"Blacks?"

"Not real black, but darker--Italian or Greek—or, in a pinch, I am sure blacks would do. He has tried to be very private, but I know a friend of a friend who has seen him at a private club outside Washington."

The old servant got up from his worn knees behind the chair; he finished with the stain and moved the broken table from the room. He had overheard many things in his time. Men of power spoke too loudly in the company of wealth and money. At one-thirty in the morning his shift ended. After working for 23 years, the servant died instantly from hit and run at the corner of Fifth and Broadway. No one noticed the type or even the color of the car. At the club the next day a collection was taken for his wife and six children, about two thousand dollars was collected.

CHAPTER EIGHT

Spring Night, 1997

Less than one hundred miles to home, and only now and then a car passed Thomas on Interstate 80. His eyes were still good for the most part. The western sky had long ago lost all of its daylight over Ohio. While the speed limit was 65 miles per hour, almost everyone on the Interstate was going 75. When the thrill and mystery of speed first came to Thomas at about five years old, it was his dad who was driving and he saw the car was going over 50 miles per hour. Of course he wanted to go faster then; and as with all teenagers, speed was a fact of life as they grow.

Then years later, in the summer of 1971, he was falling into the blacken sky of North Vietnam at three times the speed his dad would drive. Speed was not quite the same attraction after that, for there were no road maps or placards hanging for him in the heavens, other than the pictures he had seen about a week before the mission was in its final stages. That night his eyes were protected by plastic goggles and the only thing brighter than the distant flash of lighting, was the face of his watch. It was 0:200 hours when Thomas went out the Bombay hatch of the B-52 on one more mission. Some might have thought it fun, he didn't.

Even as he was falling, he didn't know where he was going. He wouldn't be told until it was time to know. It was inconsequential. Four special bullets made by the CIA lab at Fort Hood in Texas were with him. All four were packaged inside a small leaded container and he only knew of two things that needed lead packaging. Superman was one of them--he sometimes needed it to protect himself from krypton. And, then there was radiation—it, too, needed lead to shield itself from poisoning. Why this precaution and what in the universe was he going to be asked to do this time?

Falling takes a long time and the face of the man who got Thomas there appeared. His name was Bill Colby; he had been the station chief for the CIA in Saigon when Thomas was there in 1962-63. He always won approval for his far-out duty plans. He was now running covert operations from Washington. One day he showed up at Thomas's office along with Ken Opp, who was Commander of the Akron Defense Logistic for the Defense Department. Trailing behind them was the big boss G.T. Myers. The door closed and Thomas turned to meet them. G.T. spoke first as Bill held out his crooked right hand for a greeting. Thomas looked at him first and G.T. said, "An old friend, Thomas!"

"Well sir, I wouldn't say an old friend." Bill Colby's eyes squinted behind his sunglasses.

"Camp. It's good to see you." Thomas merely nodded. His old friend had become an enemy some time back. Ten years earlier, Bill Colby had sent a few hundred other men, and Thomas, behind the lines of North Vietnam. Most of them were either killed or captured and stayed. Thomas was one of the lucky ones; he made it home along with a South Vietnamese cop who he called "Bird." Their mission then was to jump into Hanoi and kill a woman Major in the North Vietnamese Army.

All of them took a seat except Ken Opp. He walked to the blackboard in the office and began listing three sentences until Thomas grunted,

"Now what?" He turned around, pulling the black leaded package from his coat pocket.

"What I am about to say is top secret Camp."

"It always seems that way sir." Ken smiled; Thomas didn't.

CHAPTER NINE

Spring, 1997

Up before dawn, Arlene mentally prepared for her six mile run on days that Thomas was not spending the night. After her second cup of black coffee, she would tie her hair back, put on her Sony Walkman and headband and be off. She had made the choice twenty years ago to be the best she could be, both physically and mentally. After the firing of her friend the gardener she knew she was all she had. So long ago that all seemed; now it at times annoyed her when people remarked about her beauty. It was all she could do at the end of each show not to try and encourage her viewer's not to take up running. She loved the solitude of her running. Yet running was more than just time alone, it was self-imposed captivity. It was the time when she was on the inside of the cage looking out. It was the odd combination of experiencing imprisonment and freedom at the same time. It was her time to plan and re-plan an hour at a time her moves to the top of her career.

The whole movement had become almost commonplace until she had met this man Thomas. She felt his life pumping though her thoughts. Was that landscape changed lately? What a sunup! Is he still in bed? Everything had changed in her walled in life. Now, she composed poems and daydreamed of him living close by.

Arlene's world was much bigger than Thomas could have even thought of. She wasted little time when she had any to spare. Today was not going to be any different; she had beaten death as many times with her travels, as he had with his. The crash of the TWA flight didn't seem to bother her as it did him. Whereas Thomas would openly bring it up as a bond, she avoided the topic. To her it was not from the jaws of hell she had come back from, it was the jaws of ever known specie of animal, from the smallest bat to the killer shark.

Privately in the pit of her stomach, the crash made her wonder about fate. Perhaps she was not in total control after all, was this why the feeling of life was fluttering inside her? Was it some metamorphosis, like the butterfly emerging from its cocoon? Was it the kick of an unborn child in her? She had found herself rubbing her stomach, acknowledging and welcoming Thomas's presence in her body.

What drew Arlene to the animal world, as a child was its own honesty. Beasts don't hide behind thin masks of make believe. Even at an early age she knew two things, animals knew what they were seeing from their own eyes and what you saw, as a person in an animal, is what you get. She discovered and soon tired of the formalities and head games humans play. She loved the fact that animals did not cover their true selves with layers of synthetic polyester, silk or cotton. It is a fact, humans learn in check out lines at grocery stores and by watching television. Where as not many people had an original thought, animals were only a meal away from their old code of survival.

What drew her audience to her was she could convey this. Many of her audience thought, she is a modern day Noah; animals seem to sense her need to belong and followed her eyes. In their element she was transported to different surroundings. In her element the animal's showed their best qualities and she always brought out the best of each to her viewing public. None of her animals cried when the plane crashed and for a moment in time, she felt embarrassed to be so closely associated with them. Were her animals aware of death and suffering, were they better off not showing their tears. Yet the answer was simple, she knew they grieved for the loss of a mate or offspring. At least the mammals did, the reptiles were not the same and their brains not as big and one or two of them could maybe even survive the crash.

She knew Thomas cried over the victims and unknown to him she did too. She cried in the stillness after he left that first morning. Many in the country jumped to all types of theories as to what took place that last few minutes as the plane was buffeted by the explosion. Was it an accident, a missile, a mad bomber? Would the animal kingdom try to blow itself to bits? The monkeys played with and protected its young. The tiger cleaned between the little paws of her cubs and their existence continued. Once she heard a statement like this, "Animals don't live…they exist." She believed that until Thomas came into her life. He and his ways made her realize, she wasn't living, she was just existing. Were fate and the two of them now so cemented together that it was the reason for her tears or could she be pregnant with his child?

For the first time in years she felt the need to love a human being, a man. She reached for her running shoes on the edge of her large office desk; the place the two of them had loved each other. Or had it been just sex and animal need? She took a small tablet from the center drawer and wrote, "If he has love to give, I have love to give back." Then she started to erase the words, worried someone may see it, and with bold black pencil marks she crossed it all out. Had she died in that plane too? What was happening to her? She wrote again, "Humans have a symbiotic relationship, give to get."

Her father had told once that he gave to the poor to get them off his conscience. She had given sex to feel love to many men, had given of her talent to get power and recognition. Had she ever felt loved? Yes… many years ago, as a child, and by the man who made things pretty, the gardener.

As a young woman when it came to men, she soon learned how to bring out the beast in them. She once said to one of her early male dates, that this behavior was fair, since men hunt and killed her creatures. The supposed superiority man assumed was beaten down by her retaliation of what she thought was fair…game. If men wanted to kill for sport, she hunted them down and broke them with her sexual charms. As she smiled to herself, she thought, "Hah, take that." The men she enjoyed beating down the most were the ones who seemed they were far removed from the world of beast. She delighted in showing them the line was thin between raw meat swinging in front of a lion and her hips moving to the passion of jazz music. When the animal came out of a man's heart she knew she was in complete control. The brighter women in her audience loved Arlene too when she made comments like, "men are driven and easily led to death by libido and lust, just the same way young Rams charge at one another, often until one of them goes off to die." In the world of cable television Arlene was the Queen Bee. She was raw and with honey dripping from her mouth she was the equivalent of any man alive.

"Watch the mother tiger clean her cubs and be reminded that she does this with the same mouth, with the gentle tongue and with the killing teeth. Watch them, do the cubs worry if the mother will forget which to use? Has there ever been a time recorded, when the mother tiger kills her own offspring?"

Arlene knew she controlled the airwaves for one hour every week as more and more humans turned her show on. She was becoming the voice of reason. "Humans sometimes forget which part of the mouth to use. I have been the victim of a cutting tongue, the careless gossip of a man dressed in a polyester golf shirt or a silk suit. God didn't trust beast with words like we have. He didn't want them to talk about how they were going to love each other. He gave us that right to use words. Now I wonder, after hearing them for so many thousands of years, if He may just be a little tired of how we honor Him with them."

Gossip had always surrounded Arlene's family from the time of her great grandparents. There were times as a child she recalled hearing the servants in the big house talk about her father and his mannerism. One day he could be so kind and then the next let one of them go for no visible reason. Then as she started to Smith College, and then on to William & Mary for her graduate work, gossip seemed to follow her every move in East Coast society. She often remembered the fools who embraced the idle talk and how they pounced on her, validating themselves by their sheer numbers. All of them like a gang of rabid dogs relishing their power on a lone red fox. She understood one clear fact about gossip--the beast is in one's human skills.

Without a spare tear she turned her attention to her animals and her career. The first time she ever broke from the script of her show was when she was doing a small feature about animals for the local NBC station in Washington. A small fire in a neighbor's garage had spread to at home where an old woman had taken in over fifty-five stray dogs. When the animal rights spokes-person was interviewed for the camera, she was so outraged that no one in the neighborhood living close to the old woman and dogs reported the fire. One of the neighbors was off-camera yelling and carrying on about how the house and dogs were a sore image on the homes and real estate.

Before long a small riot was in progress and Arlene had it all on film for the eleven o'clock news. She hit a note with the people of Washington, when she said, "The dogs couldn't call 911."

The older lady was more than likely dead of a heart attack before the fire started. God never intended for the animal's to talk. I can only assume God made Adam and Eve to do it for them. He made the two of them a scale better than the animals. One thing is for certain, He didn't make the hearts of these neighbors soft when it came to one old woman protecting so many stray dogs. It's the beast in human nature that kills."

The next day in one the newspapers, it was reported that not since the day President Kennedy was killed had so many people gone to bed sad, there wasn't a dry eye in the city at 11:20 p.m.

The white Italian leather couch on the other side of the office was cluttered. She slowly moved from the high-backed swivel chair to the armrest of the couch. The cushions were covered with all sorts of things set there for her to grab on her next flight to South America. She started to move them a stack at a time and then pushed the rest onto the floor. Lying down on the animal skin she felt Thomas's hands move up her legs from her ankles. That night after the crash the two of them had come here. Without turning on the light and with only the glow of the city, she had told him to sit down after hurriedly pushing everything to the floor.

As she undressed him he had undressed her. Thinking now to herself, she wondered if they were just animals. No! She had felt tenderness in him she had never felt before coming from all places, his eyes. She wanted him there now and made up her mind to call him after a short nap. She looked at her watch. It was eleven o'clock Friday morning. She remembered she had called to break her appointment with her therapist and fell off to sleep.

Every Friday at eleven a.m. when she was in New York she had a standing appointment with Dr. Edward Hanover. She had started visiting with him when her father found he had no control over her. At first she hated having to come into the city for the call. Now it was like seeing an old friend. The Doctor had never tried even once to be anything other than a listener. It was seldom that he even offered advice to her. She had ended her childhood on the therapist's couch and had been going there for twenty-three years. She discovered over that time some parents were people you read about in the newspapers.

They were the thieves, the child abusers, tax evaders, drug users and larcenists. They went from being mother and father to the city halls and city jails, from the protesters outside the White House to the President inside. The children don't know the difference since a child's worldview of home is strictly home for everyone, until the child leaves and discovers the next city block. That's when many of them end up on a therapist's couch. Arlene learned from her therapist that her love for animals stemmed from her distrust of her father. For a little girl who had witnessed what she had, especially a girl without a mother, Arlene considered her father a god. He let people go without a warning and turned his staff over often at his office. At home he only retained one man for over twenty-five years and that was the head housekeeper.

Once when her Jewish therapist asked if Arlene knew anything of God, she said, "No, who is he?" Dr. Hanover replied, "Doesn't your father talk about God?"

"NO, who is he?" she yelled back.

She didn't trust her father from the day she watched the gardener and his family drive out the side gate to the estate on the limestone path. They never came back to the house on Highbridge road. Arlene could never learn about the true God from her father. She just learned to fear him and his strange friends. Her father she exposed as a very insecure man who went from mourning his wife in public to almost worshiping her in private. She could not imagine a man so ruthless that he would crush her love for the gardener. It started when she felt his betrayal, when she trusted him with a child-like love. That was part of her crushed heart, but seeped so deep now, was the hidden fact, far back into the foundation of her childhood, was another deep rotten fact, her daddy had touched her childlike body too.

Her father would not accept her love secrets; he had too many of his own. He was not surprised when she ran off and eloped with the first man her father allowed her to come into contact with. Both of them hoped to escape shame. Instead she found she had married it.

Her run was almost over. "My god, this sentimentality," she thought,

"I must be pregnant, or I am in love for the first time in my life." She could see the house looming up from the earth. There was so much to try to do in life and so little time. She knew the animals didn't feel that way. To them it was one sunrise after another. There are so many animals in Thomas, I wonder if he knows? If, I am pregnant, what do I…how do I tell this child of its conception, how it transformed my existence to be the best, to only wanting to love it the most? How funny the black leather therapist's couch had been replaced with the white leather couch of love. Unconsciously she pats her belly as she turns the last three hundred yards and stretches for her remaining sugar and strength.

Running was a way of life for her. Now in her twentieth year of running, she realized it had been more than therapeutic for her slender legs and muscle-laced body. It had helped her rediscover the beauty she had witnessed as a child around her. Before she finished today she was going to allow herself the time to remember another man beside Thomas.

CHAPTER TEN

Summer, 1989

It had been eight years ago. On one of her to few visits back to Connecticut to spend some time with her mother's sister that she stumbled onto the other beauty in her life. That morning dawned quickly there, as it moved across the tops of the park benches and places where the pigeons roosted, as it dawned across the mansions and few people who were up at five-thirty. The identities of things that had been hidden in the dark of night now were bare and open. No matter what you have covered yourself with the night before, be it silk or newspaper, morning makes all stark to the eyes. The one hundred-year-old red brick clock tower bells chimed for all to awake, a familiar sound.

Roosting pigeons would soon start to flock and soar from place to place as if they too were in training. Up into the morning air she watched them go from her hotel window. Dropping their own waste on mansion roofs all over town, the pigeons missed the little targets walking below and headed north to her aunt's place.

Arlene looked down on the small park from her hotel room. Everything she saw below her had seemed to change from what she had remembered. After her father had realized she had many of her mother's features he had encouraged a relationship between her and her mother's sister Debra.

Her aunt would be surprised to see her. She had only called the house the day before to ask her aunt's maid if Debra was in town. She loved coming to the mansion of her mother's family, now owned by her aunt. Driving up from New York, the night before she did not want to crash in on her older last living relative, so she took a room at the town's local Hilton on the Square. It was never filled. She pulled down the sash of the window and the cool morning spring air bellowed in and across her skin. She reminisced about the weekends and summers she had come there as a child. In this town many thought Arlene was her aunt's daughter. Childless herself and unmarried, Arlene's aunt treated Arlene as if she were her own.

There was a very strong resemblance from the creamy complexion and strawberry blond hair. Aunt Debra was responsible for Arlene's first love for horses and her dislike for meat to eat of any farm animal. Her aunt started to call Arlene "Doctor Doolittle" because she was always talking to the animals on the dairy farm across the road from the mansion. Most of her days she was tending to the horses and spending time with the other animals.

Almost every morning right after sun-up and before breakfast Arlene would look both ways and cross to the farm. It wasn't long before the wife of the farmer was having her in for breakfast and lunch. Aunt Debra made sure dinner was with her and the social crowd she gathered with in the evening. One day she started to learn how to milk the cows, but it was reluctantly. She feared the cows hated the machines hooked up to them and that they hurt the cows. The farmer's wife assured her they did not mind and really preferred the machines rather than the human hands jerking and pulling out of rhythm. When she learned how exhausting it was for both the cows and the humans to milk by hand, she appreciated the machines. The night she had a vibrator handed to her by her first husband she automatically thought of the milking machines.

She was coming across the road one evening having slipped away from the evening party by the pool and she found a small calf tied to a post close to the backdoor of the farmer's kitchen. She went inside and told the farmer that the calf told her with its eyes, it was worried.

"Why is the small calf tied up?" She reached looking for a cookie in the red jar. The wife went to get her a glass of milk and spoke.

"We don't want her to get tough in the fields. She will be slaughtered soon for veal."

Arlene ran outside and looked at the calf, and with her heart beating hard with remorse, she told the calf; "If only I could I free you."

She swore to her aunt later that night that the calf said back to her, "I know."

Some of the other cows on the farm had names, like Andy, Mike or John. Staying for dinner one night, the old farmer said, "Mike sure was tender, not much fat on him either!"

Understanding now for the first time where her food groups came from, she put her hand over her mouth and tried to make it out the back door.

"Aunt Debra I am never going to be eating a cow again."

From that day she lived her promise and her diet became fixed and with it she could run with the best woman in the country. She put on her running shoes, did her few warm-up stretches and headed to the streets for her morning run. Running in the middle of the city she found was exciting, but not necessarily gratifying. Yet, she welcomed it with the spurt of the first light of day. The normal rural area held surprises everyday for her, the pond full of ducks and the woods where the deer would cross the road to feed.

Today instead of cows and horses she sees the tired old city and its people, too many people, all of them competing for the space her animals once held in private. Now the tall buildings block the sun and the light to make things grow. Where there was a field of lush grass now stands a building to man's ego. Too many buildings, too many people and soon the surroundings made her tense and she could not think to compose her poems that helped melt away the hours while running and the words she felt so close to.

Coming up on her right was a church cemetery; long ago filled with even more people. She had thought often of her mother and wrote of her. Only death understands before its time the concept of a lifetime. Thousands of times a day, somewhere, men and woman vow their lifetime to a dream.

Arlene was never the "Queen" of first impressions. With her history and money she didn't have to be. She was told many times a week that the world knew her and her work for animal rights. She thought, everyone knows me but Thomas, and maybe what he knows is just a side of me. I don't want anyone to know. What planet does he come from? It seemed as if neither one of them succumbed to petty intimidations. She respected him for that alone and that side of her personality which needed respect was filled. Thomas was the first challenge of her sexual existence. Coming now to the main gate out of the graveyard she tried to imagine what his children must look like by his ex-American wife.

She felt for her stomach with both of her hands and put her fingers inside the drawstring of her running pants. One of her professors told her that this was the solar plexus. Seemingly so, for she feels everything in her stomach. The world revolves around her stomach and her solar system; her emotions had been her greatest strength. For the first time she understood the vow, "till death do us part."

Arlene's legs told her it was six miles from where she had started, but the morning was still new. Rather than push herself, she slowed down to a fast walk to cool herself off and to give herself time to begin to compose in her head the letter she would write Thomas today.

"Thomas, I have eaten the whole loaf of bread, yet I feel hungry still. I feel you are the food I need to power my life forward. How do I say this any clearer? Please come help me explore the universe of my solar plexus. In her mind she crumples up the letter and watches the traffic start growing.

"People, so many people, they're everywhere", she said to herself.

CHAPTER ELEVEN

September 1970

Thomas sat listening to the sound of the air conditioner pulling the hot air from the room. He was thinking how true the statement was, that people were gathering on the face of the earth like never before. Every day the population worldwide was growing by eighty thousand people.

Thomas had seen the millions of masses in the cities of China and South American. Only a few economists held the idea of a world market in the 1970's, but by 1999 the world was worrying about the price of everything, every where. Even the old enemies of the United States, Cuba and Vietnam were trying to play up reasons for trade with the United States. The world had discovered the cost of living index. Every time Thomas picked up the morning paper, it was the economy that was driving the interest of Americans. Power, money, greed and the perception that everyone was going to live better. Everyone that is, but those people who were still being smuggled into the United States as slaves.

The door closed, as quickly as it had opened, Bill Colby, and the two men handing onto his cufflinks were gone. "Another mission", he said silently, another chance to go back to yesterday. To settle old scores, he no longer had to prove his manhood and lack of fear. The words of his Thomas's father echo in his head as he took aim.

"Just let it go, breathe and let almost all of it out, suck in air again."

The artificial high of danger and silence, the code of manhood and to self worth were trying to play a saintly tune to him. The bugle call of the charge and the trumpet call of taps made him wipe the sweat from his forehead. The air was still unsettlingly hot and the air conditioner puffed to cool the room.

The newspapers also daily covered the story of the American Air Force and Navy sending planes over Haipong harbor in North Vietnam. It was a cat and mouse game. Dodging the Sam II missiles and Russian built Mig fighters while trying blowing up the docks and mining the harbor, while at the same time, trying not to hit ships from countries like Russia or China. One of these planes was going to be ordered to drop a human cargo... Thomas... and he knew it was going to happen in just six weeks.

He was going back into the warm waters of the South China Sea. Only this time it would not be a lazy day of swimming off the white beaches of South Vietnam, but into the oil covered waters of a large natural harbor. He knew this idea of nuclear waste had been reputedly picked by the northern communists to strangle any chance of victory for the American and South Vietnamese governments. Now, the CIA was going to try to block the harbor with embarrassment, try to show the world that the North Vietnamese were lunatics and mad men, while at the same time all the parties were meeting in Paris arguing over what size the peace table should be and who should sit where.

The clock on the wall struck three-thirty. Thomas was out of his chair and heading toward the parking lot, his mind crammed with excuses he would have to give his wife for leaving home again for weeks. At dinner he ate little and pushed the china plate forward to the center of the red oak table. Sandy looked up from her plate and directly at him and spoke! "Something wrong with your supper?"

"As a matter of fact no, not at all...I was just thinking about GT Myers coming over to my office this afternoon."

"Oh, what did he have to say, you're not getting laid off are you?" He looked at her with hurt in his smile; "No I am not."

Thomas knew she had under-married. She had picked a man below her intelligence level and had tried for years to let him know it, while at the same time offering Christian love. Love for him was different than her. He wanted to seduce and play, she wanted to rest and pray. At times he saw how their three little children wore her out. Sandy did not look for sympathy. When nightly he looked at her with an evil passion and lust, she obeyed like a full-grown rag doll and soon the sex was over. After he fell asleep she would lay in their bed a few minutes, then get up to read her Bible or work on her own special projects and offer prayers to her God for them all.

"The company wants me to go to New Bedford, Mass for a few weeks."

"Why?" She said, curiously.

"Problems with production and waste." He wanted to add more, but caught himself, so as not to invent a series of lies.

"So, I guess I am left here alone again with three children?"

She rose and started to clear the dishes from the table, when Tabitha spilled her milk. There was complete silence as everyone looked at everyone else, waiting for Thomas to yell. He did not; his mind had drifted from the Sandy's figure to the milk like lighting and then to the milky cold at thirty thousand feet. He was alone, with the whole China Sea below him.

CHAPTER TWELVE

November 10, 1970

The bottom of the Swiss Red Cross airplane had been painted a lime sky blue; it would pass over, North Vietnam's seacoast from the northeast. Weekly, a flight would land in Hanoi and the Swiss government had agreed to go along with the CIA plan, when it heard of the risk to the public health of the Vietnamese people. Thomas would exit into the black night at just over thirty thousand feet, along with a unique rubber raft that he could inflate seconds before hitting the cool harbor water. Inside the raft his rifle and rations for two days.

The fabrics division at Goodyear Tire and Rubber engineered the special raft, it had no ores or would it float to the surface. It would only come up to within three inches of the top of the water. He would pull it slowly by swimming, with a special harness that he wore over his wetsuit. There would be enough air to last four hours under water in diving tanks and if he had to, he could breathe from the raft's own supply of air for six hours more. From the surface or from the air the raft would not be seen. There was but one risk of detection and that was the air bubbles escaping from his diving mask.

0400 military time and the plane started its long banking turn to the east and its slow dive. The plane had been in North Vietnam's airspace for only ten minutes. Thomas was standing next to the hatchway for the entire time the plane's pilot changed the pressure of the craft. The side cargo door was supposed to blow off and present any watching radar a dropping target. On radar if anyone noticed, all that would be seen is one object falling and the plane making an emergency run for the Hanoi airport. The hatch cover fell and right behind it was Thomas, so close, that he could have rode it down until his parachute opened tearing him away. The night was starless and overcast below the clouds, Thomas noticed once his chute deployed and he slowed that there was lighting off to the west. He could only hope that as he was Para sailing, heading in past the mouth of the harbor, the current would not carry him out. Within minutes he could see the gray ships and a few shipboard lights and smell the diesel fuel. Pulling hard to his left he passed within one hundred fifty yards of a large freighter when he noticed the dark cigar shape of the submarine entering the dock on the other side. He just had time to tuck his body into a tight ramrod when his pack of gear hit the water before him. It would have taken a miracle for anyone to notice the splash.

There was a minute when the bundle of gear pulled Thomas farther down than he had wanted to go. As soon as he could he found the pull cord and semi inflated the raft and watched it start towards the surface without going all the way up. He was chilled for a brief second even in his wet suit, maybe from the excitement more than from the cold water. There were no ifs about this, he had to find the ship as soon as possible and sink it. His head slowly raised above the water's façade. It was now raining large drops and his heart was racing as he looked across to the Russian freighter and beyond to the Russian submarine K129.

Propelled by his long, black fog fins and muscles, he gradually turned the weight of his body and played out a little nylon rope that had him tethered to the rubber raft. As far as he could see in all directions, one hundred million raindrops were hitting the water with enough force to bounce an equal drop of water three inches high, each drop only to resettle again in the bay.

Chapter Thirteen

The Pacific coast of the USSR

1970

Thomas has no way knowing that the Marshal Stalin had set sail from the city of Vladivostok on the Eastern Shore of Russia. The day was cloaked in drizzle it was almost impossible for the crew to see the shore-lined hills and green forested countryside. On the first of six days at sea the ship had been spotted minutes after leaving port by a U2 spy plane from Japan. The spy cameras shot picture after picture of the bleating smoke that was so much warmer than the sea and air around it. Thirty minutes after the time the ship dropped anchors Thomas cut away his Para sail and slid beneath the water. The Marshal Stalin was a sister ship to the freighter Thomas hoped to find. She was identical in every way to the Vladimir, a ship named after the city in central Russia. The Vladimir was still outside the waters of North Vietnam with problems of her own. She had set sail from the Black Sea and had the dangerous disadvantage of having to steam out of the Straits of Bosporus separating European and Asian Turkey. This freighter was also going to be over-flown by a U2 spy plane form the Air Force base in Turkey, but not until she reached the Mediterranean Sea.

The CIA along with the help of the Turkish government had established two places on both sides of the Straits to measure how deep the ship was in the water, thereby estimating the weight of the cargo. Also the CIA had places where they could measure the amount of radiation coming from the ship's cargo holes. Everything had been calculated, the amount of lead that was needed to protect the cargo of hazard waste from the crew and ship and even its weight.

When it was discovered that both the Marshal Stalin and Vladimir were going to be in the harbor at Haipong at the same time, some at CIA headquarters grew concerned. Which ship was carrying the spent nuclear waste? Had the Russians fooled the CIA? Only Thomas was going to be in a position to know which ship was carrying the waste. Was he going to look before he carried out his mission? It was doubtful. It went unnoticed that one of the highly placed officers at CIA was looking into what the "company" was up to. He also, bird-dogged the two ships. This man walked up to the Assistant Directors office and asked to speak with him, the secretary, after announcing him, rose to open the massive wood door.

"If I am out of place here, please tell me."

The Assistant to the Director for far-eastern affairs greeted the large man standing before him after looking at the clearance level and the photo of the badge worn by William A. Standard.

"No, no, come pull up a chair, William. What can I do for you?"

William A. Standard the Third had been with the CIA starting as a young Marine in Vietnam. He had left the Marines in 1963 after the death of John F. Kennedy. He had been wounded when some officers were overthrowing the government of South Vietnam. He was shot in the lower right leg in a shoot-out the day the President of South Vietnam allegedly died during the ruses. It was well known by now that the CIA had blessed this coup until it went sour. Then after the President was killed and not placed in exile in France, the news people blamed Kennedy and the CIA. After recovering enough to be put back on active duty with the agency, William Standard was posted to the Congo, where years of civil war threw out the Belgium backed colonial government and the African career of Standard started.

"What brings the African watch to my desk today William?"

The assistant, a small man compared to the size of Standard, repositioned himself in his large leather chair.

"We hear a rumor and I wanted to pass it on to you." What he really wanted was confirmation of what he was about to ask.

"Well, what's the rumor, maybe I can help you, if you can help me?" It seems hard to believe that at this level of the agency the top men were often left out of the loop as to what each section may be doing or investigating.

"Do we somehow have two identical ships moving from Russia towards the Pacific?" Standard wanted to dance around the question. Had this been a few days earlier he would have taken his time coming to the answer. That was one of the unwritten rules of gathering knowledge you were not supposed to have, dance with the issue and never let on you want to make love to it, don't act interested. The assistant had a little big man complex, coming to the agency out of college. He had never killed a man before and he knew Standard had killed many.

Caught off guard, he pulled a file envelope from his right-hand bottom desk drawer. Opening it in front of William alone was a breach of security, but as he was an assistant he could bend the rules and policy. He pushed two photos at William Standard and said; "Only difference it seems is the Vladimir is riding lower in the water."

Without looking up at William the assistant asked, "So what do you know of these two ships?"

William Standard knew what they were carrying in their cargo bays... enough weapons, small arms and ammunition for a small war plus "white slave women."

These weapons were heading for the communist rebels in Africa. The white slave women were heading to the United States. These women had been bought and paid for by some of the most powerfully connected deviates in the free world. They had been gathered as children from the eastern parts of Europe after the war and taken into Siberia. Watched carefully as they grew up and physically matured, they were taught English and the arts of pleasure. They had left the war-torn cities and blood-splattered fields of the Eastern block countries as young girls. Now, they were coming from the white snow- filled forests of Eastern Russia and their first stop was to be the steamy Nation Island of Madagascar. Of course they were all communists. Standard also knew the ship was ordered to keep as far from the coast of Asia as possible and to be refueled by a Russian Navy submarine tender in the middle of the South Pacific Ocean. He also knew how to keep a secret and he knew how to lie. For the first time he addressed the assistant formally. "Assistant Director, the rumor is the commies are shipping thousands of weapons to Africa, weapons we don't want to see land anywhere but the bottom of the sea."

"I sure wish we had had knowledge of this earlier. We have an old friend of yours close by. The agency sure puts a lot of faith in you older Vietnam vets," the Assistant Director said.

William Standard knew with a sharp pain in his forehead who that the old friend was at once…Thomas Camp. Due to his own bragging over the years he had often mentioned Camp to the people at the agency, especially to the younger agents. Sitting before him was this guy, a desktop type agent who wouldn't know a story from a lie. He was one of those who had yet to see real action anywhere in the world. Standard stood before him and listened to the news about the two ships converging some where in the Pacific Ocean. He felt his lips forming the sounds, and he knew he would have spoken them had he not reached for a pen in his left inside breast pocket. He caught himself as his mind wanted to race the words forward, "you idiots."

These people are needed he thought. They make the rest of us look good. If Thomas is even a stone throw from these two ships, he will see the difference and will take a closer look to find out what is in the two of them. He may even try to sink them both if he sees the weapons.

Standard walked from the office and contemplated if he should go to the office of another Assistant Director, Bill Colby and try to find out what all Camp had been asked to do. Standard, Camp and Colby had been stationed together in Vietnam in the early sixties, before the murder of John F. Kennedy and Camp went back twice after that day in November of 63. Camp had gone to private life and worked for a large corporation in Akron, Ohio. Standard had always thought Camp was being hidden there by the CIA or the NSC, but could never find records to prove this theory after about a year in and out of the hospital for a small leg wound he received from a firefight with the Vietnamese.

The day the President of South Vietnam was killed by Camp; Standard was discharged from the Marines and went to work for the company in Africa. He had only ever seen Camp once again and that was in Africa. Camp had come to the Dark Continent on orders from President Johnson to escort a Cameroon diplomat for a search to find the man's daughter.

Those were long and twisted nights, isolated times ago and Standard was glad he had almost forgotten Camp. How he had carried himself, so picture perfect, how he had looked with those piercing eyes of his. If there ever was a man called to sense of duty Standard knew it was Camp. His loyalist attitude was never an issue to the American government and Standard had heard rumors that Camp was working for the President himself.

Now, Standard was the only man who knew Camp had disobeyed his first assignment, that long ago order given to him to mark the life of a Vietnamese hooker. Standard helped Camp get her out of country and knew she was not only a prostitute, but also the top female communist spy in Vietnam. Standard was in the time and at the place where he saw what the failure to kill her had done to Camp. He saw how Camp had almost become religious after that night. It was not a fully respectable man he witnessed, but one who was indwelled with the duty to carry out every undertaking given to him with no consideration of the risk.

Standard knew so many men with so much power of information that he even came to fear his calculating of too many of the wrong things, but he had the compulsion to find out more about Camp. When something did cross his desk about Camp, it was more of the same, a supervisor, a husband and father. Not much glory here, he would think, but then again, Camp never fought for glory, he killed for country.

The killing machine Thomas had been in Vietnam was all Standard was to know, for in his lifetime, he had never met a man who could keep a secret like Camp could. He decided not to go to Colby's office without first calling him on the phone. Instead, he went to hold court, as it was his royal right to do in the cafeteria. To tell stories to some of the newest clerks and would be future spies. He loved to talk to them, watch their expressions as he told of his heroics in places like Vietnam and Africa. It was a sickness of his own making when he started to embellish the evidence, twist it around and make out he was a true hero.

The truth was he was a murderer and if someone stood in his way, he knew how to kill with ease. Where it was possible he could pull the trigger, where it was not, he knew who to go too, to get it done. Standard knew there were many men in his sordid world that for no more than a favor would kill. Today, he wished he had let Thomas die years ago rather than fallen in love with him. He should have let him go under.

Chapter Fourteen

Vietnam, 1963

The heat held everything prisoner. There was no escape from the waves it sent if you were walking, sleeping or sitting. The South China Sea and the rivers that emptied into it were just a few degrees cooler. On the coast, if you walked barefoot across the white sand, the bottoms of your feet would burn before you could cool them in the gentle surf of one inch of water. The breeze was still, like an old Southern congregation baptism. It immersed you under the heated tent top of a Sunday in July at three o'clock in the afternoon.

The men coming up behind Thomas were all his parishioners; only there was no ice tea or lemonade for them to drink, no frilly pink dresses worn by silly white females. No one was singing. They were all dressed in olive green and dark brown. Even the canteen water they carried was as hot as the air around it and it tasted like sweat. No one was so anguished as to drink the water in the streambed below, which was polluted with blood. Somewhere up ahead in the stream the water had become a warning to anything that thirsted. A violent street sign was marking the place for everything to understand, stop, look and listen to the sounds of death. From up in the foothills the water came and mixed with the mess of tangled bodies and flushed the blood from the hundreds of bullet wounds.

Thomas was the point man and stepping slowly. He was carefully picking up and placing each foot. The seven men were measuring each advancing foot by ten heartbeats and inches as they stretched out behind him for fifty feet. They were now high above the stream bank. William "Bill" Standard followed eight to ten feet behind Thomas; confident that Thomas's senses would pick up anything different in the heat of the afternoon.

The small recon patrol was looking for the left over remains of a larger South Vietnamese Marine unit that was ambushed less than an hour before. Bill turned to look behind himself and he heard the sound of the earthen bank give way. In just a matter of quick seconds Thomas was gone from his view and he heard the water splash below. The sound of the dirt and Thomas falling into the stream was followed by gunfire. He heard Thomas yelling at something he could see, at something moving in the water, trying to get away.

From his view on the outcropping of the stream, Bill could make out two figures of small people. One was running as fast as his legs would permit in the knee-deep water and the other having turned about, was ready to shoot Thomas. Without a thought or a moment of hesitancy Standard lifted his M14 rifle and started pulling the trigger. Bullets sprayed the opposite dirty bank and splashed gobs of wet mud into the air. The first of the two Viet Cong was flattened to the earth.

Aiming higher now and into the foliage of the jungle he emptied the magazine and the powerful force of Standards .308 rifle calibers tore at bits and pieces of the undergrowth. He scored a hit into the back of the second solider without even knowing it. One of the facts of the heat and jungle would take place before either of the two Viet Cong was found weeks later. The decomposed remains would be stripped of flesh in a matter of hours and the bones would never feel the pure sunshine again beneath the canopy of vegetation.

Smoke from the shooting settled like a fog on top of the water. Bill, holding on to a small palm leaned out over the edge and spoke.

"You okay down there"?

Thomas shouted back up to him just as the bank where he was standing let loose and he slid the twenty feet into the water next to him below. There had been jeopardy, gunfire, death and now laughter. Almost ever human emotion flashed like a gasoline fire in seconds. As Thomas and Bill tried to feel the rocky stream bottom and hold the other above the warm water, but most of all, for a minute, the heat escaped from their bodies. Their fear vanished in the water as one by one, the other five remaining men, jumped from the bank into the streambed and joined themselves to cooler surroundings. Then reality struggled to bring them all back to face the bloody water covering them.

This was not a swim break, not the 4th of July back home; it was the jungle of South Vietnam. Up the stream, rushing water was emptying the dead men and the water was clearing. Bill Standard with his size and strength was holding Thomas above the façade of red water. Holding him close enough to kiss him, but instead he walked him over to where he knew Thomas could touch bottom.

"Are you okay?"

"Yea…thanks, ever seen someone so dumb?"

Bill had to think for a second before he answered. "A couple of times." He looked into the eyes of Thomas, eyes like he had never seen before. He looked into eyes that were as cold as he remember his own father's eyes were. He looked into eyes that were as warm as the fever he felt brewing in the dark side of his heart. Thomas may have felt dumb for falling into the stream, but Bill felt canonized as if he had just kissed the ring of the Pope.

There was laughter coming from the young faces of the team, coming from the very men who minutes before were ready to kill and or die. Events changed that fast from the pressure of the slog in the heat. Then one by one without a word being said, the men silenced and you could hear trickling water playing along its way to the swelling river. Thomas started to move up along the steep earthy bank and Bill put his hand on Thomas's shoulder pausing him.

Bill was ready to lead, take his turn as guide and hunt for the remains of the patrol. He lingered until everyone was within whispering distance. He tapped three of the men on the head. Directing them to the other side, then up, nodding his head yes, he sent them across the open watery interval. Then he started up and out of the water, climbing and slipping, but moving toward the ridge. Bill and Thomas knew the patrol was killed caught in a cross fire as they walked along the easy route of the stream bottom. Slowly the sounds of the jungle returned and the muddy heat put back its face to the shadowy top of the canopy of green.

It couldn't be darker and still be daylight. The total picture turned to black and white. There wasn't enough light for color. The bodies were found, twisted in every possible direction. Regardless of how many times Thomas had seen death nothing prepared him for it the next time. Here even the blood was black and the day void of the hues that made his young mind think of Loony tunes and Disney. If it wasn't for the fact that there was death and infection everywhere, his mind wanted to believe it was a sterile setting that he was coming upon, until his ears heard the flies and his nose smelled the carnage. The day was old it was almost 0800 hours.

CHAPTER FIFTEEN

The House on High Bridge Road

1997

One Sunday evening Arlene stares at the phone, thinking of all the people it is connected to, yet it lies dumb and silent on her glass cherry night table. She deliberates. Is it that no one feels like connecting with her? How many people does she know? Five hundred, a thousand? She reaches over and picks up the receiver. The dial tone is her only friend right now. She punches in a number. Silence. Then calls another well-known friend. Looking around her, she sees everything she has acquired, sees what her fame has bestowed on her, things and many expensive things. With two hands she picks up one of her awards. Cold, artificial, pretend gold. Her hands warm it up, but now, it is hard, as hard as her memory the night she went to collect it. She wonders is there no end to what is wrong with me or is it the world. What a world it has become, looking around at her world of cold, hard things, but there is the couch where she and Thomas consoled each other the night of the crash. She had it moved to her house a few days after loving him on it. It is the only comfort in the room that makes her warm.

The silence reminds her of a time when she was welcomed as a young girl until her gardener friend was discharged from employment. Then she started to pay more attention to what was going on around her. When she was innocent to what was happening were the best years for her. Her father used silence as a means to protect himself from her love, but Arlene was attracted over the years toward sounds. She came to hate the muffled voices from one place to another always present in whispers in her father's home. The lull put her to sleep most nights. She wondered what grown-ups talked about, they talked so much and so intently. Very rare was the sound of laughter heard at her home. Had she ever seen her father laugh, or even smile? Knowing what she knows now, it's no wonder her father never laughed. Laughing is the music of the soul, and her father has no soul. Arlene studies her face in the mirror. "Do I smile very much?" She forces a smile, but it looks foreign to her. "I have everything, but I am not happy and have nothing!"

The years spent on her therapist's couch were a waste of time. The therapist did not make her laugh, except at the irony of her life. It was not the therapist's fault. No person on earth could mimic a father's love, kindle a mother's patience or create a soul. The beauty she knew came from the outside in. It started when the winter months surrendered the dull days to become spring and earth's rotation pulled the yellow sun higher over North America.

"So here I am, one of the most well-known women in the world, beautiful, powerful, lonely and unhappy. What the hell has all this been for?"

Arlene punches in another number to her phone. "It's been for love, I did all of this to be loved, but what good is love if I can't feel it?" She punches in a third number...silence. "Perhaps alone is all I can handle". She punches in a fourth number then a fifth. "But perhaps that was my choice." "I don't want to be alone anymore". She punches in a sixth number. "Someone wants me, I'm sure of it. It is said, there is someone for everyone, I just need to 'reach out and touch someone'." Arlene punches in the 7th number, her heart pounding in her ears, the phone slippery in her palms. The line is busy.

She picks up her gold Gross pen; it is her "real one" friend. She thinks of Thomas, wonders where he is tonight, he more than likely hates her now that he has taken the time to understand what no one else has about her. She begins to write and realizes it's to him. After finishing the letter, she feels better and hates her own softness at the same time. She thinks about how much she wanted this man and how much more, she wants to know about him. Arlene looks outside and stands and walks to the bay window and thinks, "I'll mail it tomorrow."

Four weeks pass until Thomas and Arlene meet again, this time at her home in Connecticut. They lay together giggling in her plush king size bed and she feels like it was just yesterday he came walking up the massive old stone steps and took her extended hand in greeting. The white satin curtains open to the morning dawn. Arlene watches the naked shapes of sunup resting in the window along with the realization that Thomas will be gone in just two days.

"Where is it you go, Thomas?"

Rolling on his side with some discomfort, Thomas strokes her chest with his fingers draws circles on her body as if drawing a map, he centers in on her hard nipples.

"First, I have to get in my car and drive to Ohio, I'll stop at a place called, Fred's, and make a call to one of my old friends in Washington D.C. Someone will tell me what plane to catch, and then I'll fly to this place I can't even tell you about. There will be guns and bombs to pick up and I'll be wired with some kind of device so they can trace me. I'll fly out and jump, dive deep into the ocean, plant a bomb on some boat and hopefully I will be out of the water by the time it explodes."

"You are so funny Thomas, have you ever thought about writing a book or a screenplay? You have such a mind for adventure? Will you be back by supper or next weekend?" Arlene rolls over on top of him, presses her naked body into his as far as possible. "I just can't get enough of you."

"Come on, it's all true". He pauses long enough to let the tempo of his words trail away. "Arlene, have you heard from your father lately?"

"No, why?" The mention of her father turns her love motor off and she rolls away from him. He follows, turns over to look at her and puts his hand on the sway of her hip.

"Just wondering, have you received any more letters about your life being in danger?" Arlene sits up now and brushes the hair from her face. Ever since she got the note someone wanted to kill her she's been a nervous wreck. She even cancelled taping two of her shows, wouldn't go near animals and found everyone in her production company suspect…except Thomas.

"No, but I can't go on living in fear like this. Do you think it was valid? And what do you know about death and jealous hate?

Thomas knows it was valid; he is the one who sent it. "Is there a way you could arrange for me to meet him?"

"Who…are you still thinking about my father? Why do you want to meet him?"

"Well, I am your male friend, right? I am the only one you're…doing."

Thomas smiles, shapes her lips in the form of a smile with his fingers and waits for an answer.

Arlene mood softens again, "I suppose you're right, but he's never met any of my other boyfriends, I tend to steer clear of him. The kids are coming to visit me in a couple weeks and I'll take them to visit. You are welcome to come along. I still don't know why you think he can help me."

Thomas feels a twinge of guilt using Arlene to meet her father. He is starting too really like her, but getting attached is dangerous at this point of the game.

"Ok, I'd like that. I want to meet your children too."

Arlene feels secure and content with Thomas and the fact that he wants to meet her children and her father makes her love him all the more.

"I can't wait to see you again, Thomas, I think I love you."

Thomas draws his fingers down her side from her chin to her ankles and then he cups each of her breasts to his lips. She rolls over on top of him and in minutes tries to take his body into hers once more. As she coaxes him to love her with her eyes closed, she fails to see his, wide open. She doesn't hear them, but he does, he hears the words again she spoke, "What do you know of fear and death Thomas?"

North Vietnam Waters:
1970

How long can you live in the water when your body furnace is 97.6 degrees? CIA painstakingly researched the weather over North Vietnam and said; `Haipong harbor was going to be a little warmer than normal for this time of year.' A proposal was made for a black thermo wet suit to made matters better. Checks, balances and reality! In the warm water; the differences in Thomas's warm temporary housing and the real water degrees was sufficient. Movement helped make him warmer for a short time, but in fact he was getting bone colder by the hour. The colder water would try clouding his appraisal of the need to act as soon as possible.

He moved slowly toward the freighter and made a mental note that some of the crew from the Russian sub K129 were going ashore in a Vietnamese launch. He wondered why the sub was not docked, and sat at anchor next to the freighter. His energy level was dropping and felt he should have eaten more on the plane ride in. Thomas made his way up next to the freighter and put his ear to the hull. There were muffled voices coming from the cargo bay area. The sounds were of women talking and crying. He could tell it was a lot of woman and more were coming down the pier toward the ship. Thomas slowly swam toward the stern of the ship to see what ship this was? Looking up from the water he could read the words, "Marshall Stalin." He was there to sink the "Vladimir" so he decided to wait till it was safe and then try to board the ship to see just how many women were aboard.

From under the water he could see no one was watching the launch ladder and it was only a foot from the surface of the water. He pulled himself up and made his way to one of the temporary hatch covers. Looking down he could see row after row of wooden bunks ten high filled with girls and young woman all chained some how to the bunks. He heard the sound of the motor launch coming closer and went immediately back down the ladder and floated away from the ship. Twelve Vietnamese women went up the ladder to the ship. Then the launch stirred toward the sub K129 and disembarks six crewmembers and four more Vietnamese soldiers.

The fog lifts away from the delicate yellow flowers,
They are smothered in weeds today.
The flower reaches for the heavenly sky
To kiss the sunshine
How many days do I have?
To watch this all-open outward?

CHAPTER SIXTEEN

Cuyahoga Falls, Ohio

Present Day

Garry, Bob and the rest of the morning coffee guys were all sitting in Jimmy's Café when Thomas walked in. The normal greetings took place as the edges came off the different personalities. Childhood jealousy evaporates in men friends between fifty and sixty. A real thoughtfulness for each other develops with divorce and tragedy. Many men finally learn that the communications they found impossible to have with wife's and peers becomes finally possible and all the wisdom acquired from board rooms to school rooms, from offices and shop lunch rooms finally gets a hearing after all...over coffee. Older men have so many topics to discuss in a gathering like over coffee. The subjects vary from politics, war and war's threats to women and life with or without women. Seldom does religion come up unless it's someone else's religion like Islam. No sooner did Thomas find his regular chair than David Glenda followed in behind him.

Gary was an expert on China and rubber tires. Soon after General Tire closed its doors on the Akron operations, Garry a quality manager was out of work. He contracted a position with a Jewish man in New Jersey as a VP of quality and found himself at fifty-six years old traveling in and out of China six times a year importing tries for off the road use. Bob would say he was an authority on golf and basketball. Even in front of Gary who played for Bobby Knight at West Point early in Knight's career. Gary knew the game from the gym floor up and Bob knew it from the living room couch. David was as bright a man as Thomas had ever met, but his brilliances are in building anything from city sewers to grand buildings in the downtown district. If it could be thought of, David could tell you how to do it from the basement to the radio tower on the top floor.

Thomas looked to see who was working behind the coffee counter. He called out his order as she stepped to him with two coffees in her hands presenting David and Thomas each with a cup of steaming black coffee.

Gary spoke first, "If I were twenty five again I'd ask her for a date."

"Well, when you were twenty five you still didn't know what to do with one like her. Don't forget I knew you when you were that age Gary." Bob lifted his coffee cup like he was lifting it from the floor instead of the small tabletop. Slowly it rested on his bottom lip as he watched the young woman disappear.

"And here I always thought you were a great lover of young women Gary?" David retorted with a smile.

Gary smiled a sheepish grin and said, "I have known a few."

Not to be outdone Bob butted in. "Going back and forth to China, if it were me, I would have known more than a few. How about you Thomas, how many women have you known in the biblical way?"

"I would say I have known everyone I have met." Thomas spoke without thinking first and trying to damper the conversation away from the helpless coffee waitress. He felt sorry for the young girl who had to rely on flirting with these old men for her hand full of tips. It made no difference it would take something more than intelligence to move the topic away from women this morning.

Thomas looked out the bottom of the window. The top pane was a green frosted glass to block the early morning sun, but the bottom opened wide to let everything in or out. Out the window went his thoughts back to Haipong harbor in North Vietnam. Men are always hostage to their thoughts of youth.

Haiphong Harbor North Vietnam:
1970

So much was unknown to the intelligence services about the Russian Submarines that the allied Navy had identified them only with the letter of the…alphabet…"K". He stood there much like a croupier at a Las Vegas black jack table ready to crow out at any site that may cause harm to his ship. She was a double mast sailing ship older than any ship Thomas had ever seen, maybe as old as the USS Constitution in Baltimore Harbor, Maryland. Thomas had a slight panic wondering if the lookout may have seen him. Could he even afford the chance? He had to do something and he had to do it fast. He pulled a small contact mine from his underwater pack and sunk down to the bottom of the K129 submarine. Three days later the submarine sank in the deep Pacific Ocean.

Akron, Okio:
August, 1961

Between the steep banks of the railroad tracks were 50 steps to go down or climb, the old rail station had been built before the turn of the century. The tracks ran east and west, but out side the city limits, the tracks turned north and south. Paris Island Recruit Station for the United States Marines was South, a day and a half by train away. By 1961 the steps had become loose from thousands of feet taking tens of thousands of steps. As the pointed cement holding them in place loosened and cracked from tons of salt spread to melt the winter snows and ice. Every few feet a naked electric bulb on a black rod iron post attempted to light the way and the tall green weeds waved like the American flag set the top of the white rail station house.

From the time of World War I to the war in Vietnam, thousands of men and women left this station to fight and serve the United States. The odd smattering of truth was that hardly anyone other than the family or friends of the service people remembered or knew the rail station was even there any more. The Super Highways and Airports had become the avenues for transportation travel in America.

Today, it was a Northern Ohio winter day in February.

At the top of the 50 steps over looking the ravine were four old green wooden benches. Thomas sat there with his pen and yellow tablet and started to write a letter to his children. He seldom went any where with out either pen or paper to write on. Looking into the February sky to the north he could see February had one more snow storm to deliver to Akron, Ohio. The weather was changing from pleasantly warm and the wind was pushing hard to enter his jacket.

"So, children…where and how do I set in motion all I want to tell you and thank you for? Do I start here, where I left home many years ago, he said to himself?

When I was a young boy I wanted to be a writer. I always loved to sit at my daddy's feet and listen to him and his six brothers spin their tales and stories. All of them could have been writers.

After all, writers know everything! By the time I came home from the Marines at nineteen years old, I wanted to be a writer and a poet. I was sicken of the war and it's to colorful face. I was certain the Angel of death had saved me from die a death just once, to die a little each night. There is no salvation in death, it is only possible if you live.

The problem was I did not know anything. As I read and fell in love with words, I discovered that poems could be books in themselves. Now, at this age, I have just one novel published, but I have an abundance of poems to share with you. It takes me years to write a novel, but poems come into my mind every day. I like to look at a face; much like an artist does, and then sit down and write a poem for that face. So, there are poems in this collection that I could have written just for you".

His oldest son has married a Russian woman, who he considered so sweet. Sunday, the three traveled to sell their sailboat on Lake Erie. Along the way Lena, the mad Russian daughter in law said, "Poppa Kemp, why do you not look for a Russian lady like me…?

"Well, she humbled me, because I said…" Lena, you are beautiful, but I wonder if a Russian lady could keep up with my mind?" So, she said, "Papa Kemp Russian women on the average read more, study harder and long for a man like you with brains and kindness."

Thomas sat and thought. "I do not find a bit of fault in wanting to stay invisible, but she knows me so fast and in a short period of time. She has me wondering...who is this Russian woman? Do I want to know? Sure I do, but I know you can not pry the invisible from the heart of a woman, she in good time will show her nature with her words.

Ted, my young son is 33...still in college and working full time. I told him he could stay until he is finished with school, did I do him a favor?

Tabitha my only daughter is a manager with Fed Ex and

just at 35; she has finished her Masters Degree at Kent State.

Thomas, Lena's husband and my oldest is 37 and a Director of Instructional Technology and Support at Ashland University. He is working on a Doctorate Degree Urban Education Communications.

I never knew what was expected of me when I walked down these steps and headed for the Marines. I am at the rail station beside the University of Akron, not far from E.J. Thomas Center. I was not prepared in so many ways to face what I was baptize to do. The only reason I did not fall short was because of the iron will of my father. I would not disappoint my father, just like none of you have disappointed me.

When he let me go at just 17 years old; I came to realize it was all most impossible for him. When my oldest son Tom left for the Army back in 1988, I had a feeling for what my own dad must have felt. There was this feeling at night that Tom would walk through the door and be home for good.

Many would say when I left for Marines at seventeen I was already suffering from PTSD. And, sure the service connected years and war compounded all of it. There is only one thing I am miserable about while I performed my duty and that was for sinking the Russian Submarine K129 and killing the men in her.

When I look at Lena and see her Russian roots and know one day she will give me a grandson and granddaughter I sink too and hate that part of my past.

CHAPTER SEVENTEEN

Some where in the middle of the Pacific Ocean:
1970

I was not there, but in my dreams I could see the fist of water pouring into the small hole my contact mine made into the K129. Then the melon shaped hole expanded and all that I could have wanted happened as the hole grew and grew. K129 finally submerged for the last time and the projectile hole was weak enough that the pressure of the dive could not be stopped and her skin tore like flesh. Little did I know that my duty became my misery and my obsession for victory became my personal defeat?

Abe Lincoln had said it at Gettysburg, "what happened here will not be remembered…but it was. Shakespeare who had promised the Friends, Romans and countrymen…that the evil men do is oft remembered, but only if all of them are not dead, was right. Everyone in K129 was dead and the Russian sailors really did swim with the fishes. So, my Februarys were to be remembered and the shortest month of the year was to become my longest month every year. "Little Russian grandson and daughter to be, forgive me I did not know we would sing and dance on the edge of the Volga River one day, forgive your old ugly Grandfather".

The miles rolled by and he half listened to Lena and Tom talk on about the money selling the sailboat would free up for their new home on the mound. The distances evaporate like the old days of life and his musty cigarettes. The times had changed but the world remained the same as yesterday and in his head he composed a new poem.

"How could I have misplaced my heart again?
Clearly I remember,
I sat it down on the waters edge while watching you sail way.
The waves began to crash ashore.
And nearly up rooted the dock I scrutinize from.
I looked and it was gone
The water and wind indiscriminate
Oh, the storms you created in my mind.
Displacing every love I thought I ever felt.
Then at midnight every part of me was alone again
My mind vacant, my heart empty, my blood drained.
Come quickly dawn."

Many a man has lost everything to the slave he makes of his passion. Men have seized a right over other men as far back as ancient times and the first of mankind, a false right, yet a right garnished from strength. With this right men steal the women of other men and the children of nations and turn them inward to strengthen a despondent ego. Life has been a power house of goodness and courage for many men and women and life has been a preacher's voice falling on deft mute's ears to others. Regardless of the seasons and years, life has this impossible work in partnership and it is to go on, to live to tell the tale, write the story...take a breath, go on take another. Tell the story as clear as feasible...paint the picture.

Chapter Eighteen

1990
Miami, Florida

It looked like any other ship lying next to the many piers in Miami harbor, all except the cruise ships, but he knew right away he had been on it before. The cruise ships are the giants of ocean going vessels and they look like floating skyscrapers. The rain was making the night even darker as I got out of my taxi and headed up the gangway to the main deck. Across the way, another ship was getting under way to move out with the high tide. Right behind me the harbor pilot came running up the steps, so I wasn't the last person to board. As he passed me going to the pilot house he spoke and looked at me. I am sure he wondered why I was so late; I almost missed the departure.

As I took the last step, a man I assumed was the officer of the deck spoke to me saying, "Welcome, Mr. Kemp?" his voice forming a question after he pronounced my last name.   I could hear Celine Dion's voice singing a soft song and I turned and met two of my shipmates playing their "Sony Walkman's" and standing against the white iron railing. The young man, maybe thirty five, reached out his hand and said, "Frank Cutter, and this is my wife Marie. You must be Mr. Kemp?"

"Yes I am, and it's nice to meet you both. We all smiled and then one of the ship's crew came up to me, took my bags and said with an accent, "this way Sir."

From the time you entered the inside of the ship, everything was freshly painted; steel bulkheads were broken up here and there with fabrics, paintings, and a sea of red crimson carpet. I was caught off guard by how nice the atmosphere was. I remembered thinking this was not the ship that Humphrey Bogart sailed on in some of his movies from the nineteen forties and fifties, that depicted old rust and smelly damp.

The crewman took me to the door of my cabin. The door was opened and I almost thought there was some mistake; this must be the Captain's room. It was beautiful and evenly decorated in lime and shades of blue. The only thing I noticed, that was not what I expected, was the size of the bunk or bed. It was just a little bit bigger than a single bed. I knew why; I had asked for an extra table to be put in the cabin for my papers. I love to spread them out as I write and read.

I felt the ship's engines start and heard the ship's horns as the loud speakers sounded off. "Make way for sea," said someone up on the bridge. I looked for my camera and went back up the few steps to the railing and watched as the lines were gathered and unhooked from the pier. And we were off to South Africa, our next stop, and already I had an idea for a poem.

> Across the deep green sea, waves toss sound
> Never the less the unfathomable silence of the shadowy water
> The Humpback Whale calls out for its mate.
> Not a single other sound or voice can be heard but its own.
> Until the answer emerges from deeper waters and still places
> "I am here remembering you, come let us touch?"
> She slides up next to his bulk and his eyes watch her surface.
> Southern blue warm skies today
> Watch the two of them below as they swim north.
> She says, "Yes, I am remembering."
> And she is protected.

We cleared the harbor and the harbor pilot was picked up by a slick smaller boat that took him to his next duty. It was 0100 in the morning of the first day. I wanted something to eat and noticed a large white sign with red letters welcoming passengers aboard, listing many things. Near the bottom it read:

Galley Hours- for Guests and Crew
0500 – 0630 Breakfast
11:00 – 12:00 Lunch
19:00 – 21:00 Dinner
11:00 – 12:00 Mid-Night Lunch

Then in smaller letters, spelled out my delight: Best Coffee in the World – Anytime "Welcome".

Looking at my Seiko watch I noted it was too late for midnight lunch, so coffee would have to do. The easy bobbing of the ship had started after we sailed south by southeast and the sea was like glass. The rain had stopped and the moon was fully reflected off the smooth water.

Again, I could not believe my eyes as I stepped into the ship's galley. Everywhere there were clean, white table cloths over solid oak tables with matching high back chairs, which I observed were not upholstered. Three tables for six people and one table for eight shined from old world cleanliness. Large white china mugs hung from hefty brass hooks, close to the polished steaming copper coffee pot. One of the mugs had my name on it. I had to smile, when on the one upholstered leathered chair in the room I saw a sign made by the same sign maker: "As Captain, I am always on duty and do not have to remove my Cap." Being a cap wearer, I fully understood what the captain was saying and had to smile as I drew down a black mug of steaming coffee.

No sooner had I sat down and put the cup to my lips when a small, smiling Latino man came to my table from the kitchen area. "Señor, would you like some of my best cherry pie?" His name tag read: Antonio.

"Yes Antonio, I would love some." Frank and Marie Cutter stepped through the door: a hatchway in nautical terms.

"Hello again," he spoke with a smile. She looked at me and then turned away saying, "Hi."

"I see you found the coffee and pie." Trying my best to show my manners, I nodded and smiled broadly.

"Yes, and it is as advertised, the best coffee in the world." An almost too friendly guy, I said to myself, and she is a shy dorky gal.

Avoiding any more eye contact, I drank my coffee and ate my pie so fast it burned all the way into my stomach. As I excused myself and started out the door, there was another sign and a picture: "NO SMOKING," and a curious picture of the entire crew and the Captain. He was smoking a red bier pipe.

The next morning as Thomas was dressing for the new day at sea, there came a knock on the door.

"Just a minute, be right there."

"No need Señor, the Captain says to tell you come for coffee to his cabin before breakfast."

The Captain greeted Thomas at the door to his own cabin resembling a house in Sparta. It consisted of the bare necessities for the few hours a day he spent there. The one thing that Thomas noticed right way was the size of his ham radio and the coffee mugs. Then there was the desk on which the ship's log book was securely chained, but, with a slight push of a small brass catch the book would come off the chain.

Captain Lafontaine was as Thomas had remembered him, older, but still the quick spirited and small man he was when Thomas first met him back in the 1970's. At that time Lafontaine was the first officer of a commercial fish processing boat that sailed the Northern Pacific Ocean. He himself was not a fisherman but a Merchant Marine Graduate of the United States Merchant Marine Academy and a spy for the NSA. His task was to keep the old rusted Japanese flagged ship in international waters and away from the clutches of the Russians, Chinese, and North Koreans. He was the officer in charge of finding and pulling Thomas from the waters off the coast of Haiphong harbor, North Vietnam.

"Captain Jack, how are you?"

"Come in Thomas, join me and tell me why you're sailing with us this time; if you can tell me."

Captain Jack was what Thomas first called Lafontaine, as he reached for the life ring Jack tossed from the process deck where the overpowering smell of fish guts came from.

Captain Jack Lafontaine was six years old when he went to sea the first time with his father and grandfather. Both of the older Lafontaine men were lobster fisherman who lived on the most eastern shore of Maine. This is where the sun came first over the United States coastline --- in Eastport, Maine. From that day until he entered the Merchant Marine Academy, every chance he got to go to sea with the older men, he went. With his school books in tow Jack would rush from school and head for the boats and harbor. The affectionate words he heard as he came on board the Boston Whaler lobster boat to start helping with the catch was, "Is your school work done?"

When Jack was sixteen and his grandfather died he made Jack's father promise to bury him at sea. Jack had piloted the boat out the eleven miles to lower the old man's body into cold winter sea. Jack's grandfather had always smiled and assured his son and grandson he would not be eaten by the lobsters, he was too tough, but still he wanted the sea to be his cemetery.

CHAPTER NINETEEN

Somewhere off the Coast of West Africa:
1990

"Many Greek ships have a goddess' name. I read a short history of the one I was on, from the silver plate on the galley bulkhead. The ship I was on, the "Olympians," was the company once owned by Aristotle Onassis. Before that, the Merchant Marine Association of the United States owned it. It traded hands after the last flight of Americans left Vietnam."

I recall a saying credited to Aristotle Onassis: 'If women didn't exist, all the money in the world would have no meaning,' and I agree," Thomas exclaimed, as he sipped his coffee, listening to Captain Jack tell his story of what had been his darkest hour at sea.

The ship was being pushed from behind by the southerly winds and making up time. Most people naturally liked being around the Captain, his behavior was unproblematic and his leadership accepted by everyone. Thomas could understand why men would follow him across the oceans of the world. Had Jack been an astronaut, men would have followed him to Mars; fear was alien to his character. The Captain pushed a plate of coconut cookies over towards Thomas.

"The cook harvested the coconuts himself from a beach in the Solomon Islands, try one." Thomas took a cookie and could not believe how tasty they were. The Captain pulled a Pall Mall cigarette from his white shirt pocket, lit it from a gold cigarette lighter, and began to speak again.

"Years ago when I was very young I met a girl on my return from my first ocean trip."

Thomas spoke up looking at the Captain eyes. "How old were you then Captain?"

"I was twenty years old, forty years ago."

"Did you ever marry her?"

"No, she threw me over-board by the time I returned the next time to Maine. If she had not, I would have settled for her doing anything, but not running off with some crab angler. My family could not take the insult, since then I have known far too many women, none of them very faithful. What was odd my mother and dad were married 63 years, before mom died".

Jack fell silent and sipped his coffee.

For reasons only Captain Jack's subconscious knew, he was ready to trust this fellow voyager. The Captain, like us all, had a story to tell. Looking into Thomas's eyes he was sure Thomas would understand his reasons for his nightmares. He dipped a fresh cookie into his coffee, never taking his eyes from it.

As Jack paused with his narrative, Thomas thought to himself about his childhood friends. Some as old as Jack, men who spent more time reflecting about their past sins, instead of planning more, for the time they have left on the earth. The time in youth when life's stylus records soon become useless, worn and broken, man's designs never fully executed. Man's dreams become a revolving nightmare and Thomas can see Captain Jack is midway into his own frightening.

Captain Jack looks at Thomas; he thinks he sees a man much like himself. An adventurer and a man who fought for what he thinks was right, but Thomas has learned that right is not always the sum of what others find to be true. Right is the subjective and not affected by the external, it is always the underlying truth and it is debut in the word of God. In Thomas's mind, a musical composition begins with a missed note on a baby grand piano, while the Captain speaks again.

"After my duty on the ocean tugs, the CIA put me to sea once more, that's about the time we first met in the pacific. I was sure about what we were trying to do as we gathered intelligence shadowing the Asian coast line of Russia, China and North Korea. When the North Korans grabbed and boarded one of our Navy ship's, I could not understand why we just did not go in after her, but I kept my mouth shut and thought to myself the President knows more than what I do. Yet, as each embarrassment came to pass, I was sure I could do a better job, but you know yourself, no one was going to give me the chance."

Thomas nodded his head and Captain Jack continued.

"When Howard Hughes teamed up with the CIA to salvage the Russian Sub K-129, the one I know Thomas, you sunk, somehow, it went down the same week we picked you out of the Pacific. My station chief approached me to be the First officer on the ship, "Glomar Explorer". Of course Thomas, you know the whole salvage failed after the sub was on its way up and then broke in half?"

Thomas looked at Captain Jack and said, "Yes, so we are told!"

"What do you mean; so we are told? Do you think the mission worked Thomas?"

"Captain, I know you have heard the term "plausible denial," some say that was the beginning of the end of the cold war."

"Yes I have heard that and it makes sense to me because after that there was an increase in our efforts to gather more and more intelligence. It was as if we could not stop and money was no object nor cost to high. That is what make me realized our weakness Thomas. We had the money to spend to ring the Russians with spies in the sky and under the ocean, but not the money to protect the Lobster beds off our own shores. My own dad was struggling just to make a living at what kept him and my mother alive. We had millions to spend to bring up a rusted piece of junk from the ocean grave and nothing to help my people carve a living from the sea. You know Thomas the Constitution says we the people of the United States, in order to form a more perfect Union."

Thomas looked at Captain Jack's shirt pocket and noticed his gold Gross pen and said, "Captain, you know before it speaks of the promotion of the general welfare it says, establish justice, provide for the common defense, these have to be met before the government can give out welfare checks. Without our freedom, we have no nation, and the men who live outside the law, always find that they really have no justice themselves."

We could debate this all night; you have acted outside the law."

"Yes, I have, but never outside the code," Thomas quickly defended.

"What code? I read a lot and I went through the same orientation that you did at the company store. What code, Thomas? Some code you read about on the back of a cereal box, where you found your "Sky King" ring?" The Captain was agitated either by Thomas' mention of the code or by his own sub climax; he wondered if he should just stop now, or go on and let Thomas hear of all the hell that he had been a part of working for the country.

Suddenly, he seemed to "let it go" and reached to pour some more coffee. As he watched the heat swirl up from his coffee mug, he started to talk again.

"Thomas, you and I did not go to those Ivy League schools, where money begot money and money made friends with more money. We came up the hard way by doing what those money bastards wanted us to do and do not tell me what they wanted was always for the good of the country."

"Are you sure it was the company you were working for, Captain? Or could it have been just for some powerfully sick men, or even just for yourself," Thomas asked although he already knew the answer.

"Why would they have me sail half way around the world and bring poor white women slaves into a country that the constitution secured liberty for? I will tell you the answer, for greed and profit, for prostitution and evil pleasures," Captain Jack answered, pretending to have a shred of decency.

"How can you say that, Captain, when you have Frank and Marie Cutter sailing with you too?" Thomas knew what their presence on the ship meant, but he questioned the Captain, nevertheless, giving him every opportunity to redeem himself.

"Thomas, he is a Doctor and she is a nurse, and they're going to try to keep our returning passengers alive on the trip back to the States." Captain Jack hesitated for a moment; like Judas may have counted forty pieces of silver, he imagined himself counting the profits.

"They're just here to make sure the profits are capitalized," said the Captain referring to the Doctor and his wife. "It's for everyone's benefit." Captain Jack raised his lowered eyes with his jaw slightly dropped open, as if he had just seen a ghost. "What do you mean by that, Thomas that you must be on this ship at 'their' order, and no one travels to Africa by ship, when they can fly?"

In an instant like a flash of lighting, from across the horizon, Thomas stood up, grabbed the gold cross pen from the Captains shirt pocket, and boldly stated, "Here is the code: An eye for an eye, a tooth for a tooth, and death for a murderer." The Captain, startled for the first time in his life revealed fear in his eyes. With that, Thomas plunged the pen into the Captain's right temple and left it there.

From the reflection of the steaming coffee pot, Thomas caught sight of the Cook Stewart, "Antonio" coming at him with a meat hatchet. Thomas grabbed the pitcher of steaming coffee and threw it in Antonio's face. This stopped the attack long enough for Thomas to pour some more hot coffee on Antonio's hand as the hatchet dropped to the deck sliding toward him. Thomas picked it up and with one toss imbedded it into face of the attacker before he could scream.

Quickly because neither man was dead, Thomas hoisted them over the railing and into the early morning sea. There was no time to recover or reflect. There was only the tasks ahead and the rest of the crew to kill along with Doctor Cutter and his new bride. Time grew short, the ship still hurried toward the harbor and the harbor pilot was just across the open water less than ten miles away.

To be continue in 2015 by Thomas T. Kemp.